Vengeance

Barbara Winkes

For D.

Chapter One

I say *I Do* on a rainy Thursday morning, to everyone's surprise including mine. It feels like a strange dream, pleasant, but strange. Up until this moment, I might have thought there could be an alternative, or something that needs to happen first.

But it's here. Listening to the officiant's voice, I study the faces of our guests. Mom and Dad, my colleagues, my boss. Sofia, Claudia, Anna. Cousin Luca's wife declined the invitation. It's understandable given the fact that together, we put Luca behind bars.

We make a good team, even with the inevitable secrets. It makes sense. Doesn't it?

"It's time," she whispers to me, amused, because I've been drifting. "Kiss the bride and all."

She leans in, and just like that, for everyone to see, I'm Mrs. Kendall Mancini.

No, it's not like that. I'm keeping my name. She does have a way of taking me over sometimes, and I like it too much. After a kiss that feels a bit too intimate considering the audience, we accept congratulations.

My parents hug me. "This is an odd twist of fate, but you're happy. That's all that matters."

"You look beautiful," Mom adds, her eyes welling up, not for the first time today. They are no strangers to the story, at least, most of the story. That makes it more real.

"Thank you."

I look over to Kendall who catches my gaze. She stands with Sofia Bianco, a woman Kendall's parents once rescued from an abusive marriage with a rival family's son. I know she wishes they could be here now, to see everything she's achieved.

On the street, they don't call her princess any longer. Some call her a rat. She was able to keep her business together while providing us with information on some of the worst criminals haunting the city. I owe her, privately and professionally.

Who cares about a few secrets and surprises? We were meant to be.

"Congratulations, Agent Johnson."

My supervisor, SAC Carr, shakes my hand with a polite smile. It's not just out of friendship that she's here, and the same goes for my colleagues Ryan and Hampton.

We had to find a way to move forward. This was the best possible one.

Worst case scenario, I can refuse to testify against her, not that I see myself in that situation anytime soon. Kendall has accepted (or been gently convinced) to take a part-time job as a consultant on certain cases.

"Thank you, and thanks for coming."

Carr acknowledges my words with a wry smile before she greets my parents.

"Have a wonderful day. I'm afraid I'll have to leave."

"I'll see you on Monday," I say. It's not going to be a long honeymoon. There are too many things we still have to figure out.

"You only took the weekend off?" Mom asks.

"Too much work I'm afraid. For both of us." Kendall, who has joined us hugs my parents as well. "We're going to make this a memorable day."

Dad and Kendall's late father, Alphonso Mancini, had history. It makes things easier and more complicated at the same time. He's well aware of the power this family once wielded, and everything that came with it. An odd twist of fate, he's not wrong about that.

"It sure is," he says. "If you need help with the move, just let me know."

"I think we got it covered." Kendall smiles. "Even though your daughter took me for several million...but what can I say, I love her."

"So she went easy on you?"

"Blake," Mom chastises. She and Dad have been together so long, she is well aware of everything that's spoken in and between the lines.

Kendall is always testing the limits. I have accepted that it's something that will never change. What can I say? I love her. Call it odd, or whatever, but it's true.

"Don't worry. It's fine, and he's right. I'd like to think that it was both my smart business practices and Robyn's mercy, but we're good. It's all paid off now, and my records are clean."

I think she's just as surprised as I am at the flash of emotion on Dad's face.

"That's something Al always hoped for," he says, referring to his childhood friend, who went on to become head of a crime family. Before Kendall, Alphonso had struck a deal with the FBI, but he never lived to see the results of it.

"I'm glad to know that's what he and my mother wanted—even though it cost me a lot of money."

Mom pats her back. "I think you can afford it."

"I can. We'll all meet for lunch in a bit?"

She takes my hand and together, we leave the courthouse, stepping outside into the pouring rain where the driver waits with a dripping umbrella. Rain on the wedding dress. I'm so far beyond believing in bad luck it barely registers. A lot of bad things happened. We're due for a break, even if it's just for a few days.

"You've been quiet," Kendall observes when we are in relative privacy, just us, and the driver in the front. "You're not worried about my ability to provide for us?"

"Funny. I'd like you to remember that I still have a job. No, I'm not worried."

"About anything?"

"No. I swear." I pull her close to me, ignoring the other person in the vehicle as they ignore us. I need to anchor myself in this new reality, and this is the best way to do it.

"If this is a preview, I look forward to the wedding night."

It's true. We paid our dues. We're free—relatively speaking.

The reception takes place at *Catania*, the Mancini family restaurant that was founded by Kendall's great-grandparents. If these walls could talk, they'd have many stories to tell, some charming, some disturbing. The infamous back room is now used for storage. Today, no troubling conversations take place. Everyone is all smiles and laughter. It's a bit cozy for a wedding, but we are keeping it within family. There's room for everybody.

I can't help thinking of the first few times Kendall took me here.

Her cousin Luca was present at times.

And Jimmy Bruno, for many years Al's right hand man until he decided he was owed more, Alphonso's daughter and a bigger chunk of the business. Bruno is serving a life sentence for murder, attempted murder and a host of other crimes.

"Memories?" Kendall asks beside me.

"Ghosts," I admit.

"Nothing that good food and wine can't make go away."

"Can't wait to try."

She brushes her fingers over my cheek, making me shiver in anticipation, the thought of food vanishing.

"Then let's do it."

"Thank you for having me. I have to admit, I was surprised to get the invitation. It was a beautiful ceremony."

"Thank you for being here," I return when Sofia comes to talk to me late.

"How times change," she says. "I'm glad Kendall found you. I wanted to ask you something quickly."

"Sure. Anything." It's a wedding. The subject matter won't get too tough.

"I wonder if you know why Kendall gave me what's basically her job in the company. Not that I'm complaining, and I'm determined to do the best I can. I always thought that if it comes to this, it would be Claudia first. She's younger...and she's family."

"You are family too. Never doubt that. Kendall gave you the job because you earned it."

That's all the explanation I can give her. She squeezes my hand with a smile. "Enjoy every moment."

Is this what it's going to be like? I wonder. I had no idea Kendall was making changes this big at the Mancini Group. After the long-term investigations into her business, she had to pay hefty fines. She never told me that she was going to step down as CEO. What does that mean? The consultant job won't make up in hours or money what she'll invest to carve out that position for Sofia. If I learned something about Kendall, it's that she doesn't do idle.

What is the plan?

The question follows me all the way through the excellent meal, the toasts and speeches. Kendall, next to me, looks happy and proud. Perhaps I should leave it at that. It might not be anything significant. Sofia came to me. It's not a secret. Or is it? I drown my fleeting doubts in chianti and champagne. The 4-tier tiramisu cake is topped by two brides made of delicate sugar art. Just like life, I think. Delicate. We brought down a crime boss, his family and cohorts, including a judge.

Why can't I chase the feeling that the worst is yet to come?

Chapter Two

There is pride in something other than the bottom line. This has never been so true to me as it is at this moment. We've moved on to a more private celebration, lust and leftover cake with champagne. I wasn't embellishing. These things do make everything better.

Robyn, who has been tense and pensive for days, is warm and relaxed in my arms.

"See? I'll always take care of you."

She's humouring me, for once foregoing the return. I'm not ignorant. I know she can take care of herself and has done so long before I came along. It's more of an indulgence. After parting with a substantial sum of my money I think I deserve it.

Turns out that after the deal, the FBI still has use for me. It's both fascinating and disconcerting, but since I started on this path a while ago, I see no reason to stop.

"You took care of Sofia too," Robyn says. I saw them talking earlier. There's no point in denying it.

"She's family."

"That's what I told her. I'm curious though. You want to step away from the company? Is that temporary?"

"I haven't decided yet," I say, running my fingers down her bare arm. "It's not a big deal. I'm going to need some time, and, as you know, I also took on a new job."

"Expert consultant on organized crime," she muses. "That's a far cry from running away for good."

"You refused to come with me. I had to look into alternatives."

She turns to look at me, her expression somber.

"There's talk about you."

"I expected that. We've made a lot of waves out there. I'm not afraid," I add when I realize she's waiting for more of an explanation. "The people that got busted won't be out anytime soon. If anything, it's a lot safer now. There will always be danger. It's been with me all my life."

Given the line of work she chose for herself, I'm not sure how to interpret Robyn's gaze.

"That's not news to you, is it? You said yes, so I'm afraid there's no going back."

Robyn chuckles. "I'm not afraid. But I'm wide awake now. Should we get some more champagne?"

When in doubt...

"That's a brilliant idea. I know what else we could do."

The light-hearted moments have always been few and far between. We had better cherish them while we can. Right now, there's nothing immediate to worry about. If it should come to that...Robyn knows that whatever happens, I always have a plan B.

—◦◦◦—

Friday morning, I set the table in the kitchen and order our breakfast. It arrives before Robyn walks into the room, wearing only boxers and a tank top.

"Good morning, Mrs. Mancini," I say, jokingly, because it's not entirely true. I just like the sound of it. She walks into my arms.

VENGEANCE

"Agent Johnson to you." Robyn enjoys the play as well. "Do you have to go to the office today?" she asks.

"Save for any emergency, I can handle things from home. Which means we can pretty much resume where we left off."

Robyn steps back and, with a grateful smile, accepts a cup of coffee.

"Evading tricky conversations with food and sex?"

"We've been doing it since the beginning. It works, doesn't it?"

"Sure does," she agrees. I lean in to put my lips to her neck, feeling her gasp. "I'm tempted, but I think I need food first."

With some regret, I let her sit and start uncovering the dishes.

"As you wish." She's right though. It looks amazing, and we're going to need it. We can't be without each other, yet there is a handful of subjects we better evade.

Sofia unwittingly forced my hand. I'll have to think of something.

Robyn seems to be a tad distracted at the abundance of food which makes me smile. It also gives me more time to come up with a strategy.

"We both know that the job is the FBI's way of keeping tabs on me. For what it's worth, I don't care, but yes, I do want to take a step back and see where we are. Sofia knows the company inside out, the way it used to work, and the way it's supposed to work now. I could forgive Claudia, but she's too close to Luca, and people are aware of the history."

Robyn listens, absorbing the information. "You think you have more street cred?"

"Well, I've always been playing in the big league, bigger than Dolan and his ilk. They don't care so much about street cred as long as someone can deliver the money or the product. In my case, real estate, properties, and such."

"I'm not sure why they called you princess. That never felt right. They should call you queen."

"Yes, finally someone's acknowledging that!" I say and we both laugh. "I didn't keep anything from you. The company is still affluent, and as long as the FBI and IRS aren't seizing all of it, we can pay Sofia's and everyone else's salary and still have a fairly comfortable lifestyle. I don't see how they would come after me now. I paid for my freedom, and I made heads roll."

"You did," she acknowledges, sounding amused. "Like I said, queen."

"Yes I am." I raise my glass. We'll continue with the champagne, why not? "Happy first day of marriage," I say.

"Same to you. So far, it's been everything I could have hoped for."

Her words fill me with unexpected joy, and perhaps predictable, almost feverish anticipation. Who would have thought? When she asked me to marry her, for a few suspicious seconds, I thought she might be making fun of me. Our relationship defies all reason, though we always manage to somehow meet in the middle.

"I'm glad. There's more to come."

<hr />

After a couple of days of married bliss with Robyn, I have to leave her at home to take care of a few business-related items on my list.

"It won't take long," I promise. "I'll be back sometime this afternoon, and we'll have the rest of the day."

"It's okay. I'm aware you still have obligations that don't include me—and I won't be looking over your shoulder 24/7 any longer."

"Good. I'll see you later." I lean down to kiss her, Robyn, my wife. I didn't miss the flash of suspicion, only for a split-second, when I told her. I can't blame her either. We didn't start out with a foundation of trust.

I take my own car this morning and drive all the way to the state prison. I'll have time to get back, get lunch and make my 2:00 p.m. meeting. At the prison, I'm surprised when they lead me to the visitors' area right after I've put my bag and cell phone into a locker. I didn't expect it to be so quick, but perhaps it's better that way.

Luca gives me a hard stare, but he sits down across from me. Seconds tick by in silence. I shouldn't feel guilty at all. He teamed up with a murderer and drug dealer for a side hustle, and he could have destroyed everything, for his mother and sister, for all of us.

"So, you finally came to gloat."

Figures. "I just wanted to see how you're doing."

"Why do you care?"

So far, this is pretty much going the way I expected. I'm already feeling less guilty. I had to do this, of course, pay my dues. Nothing more, nothing less.

"You're still family. You did something beyond stupid, granted, but your family. That is why."

"Did you go see Jimmy?"

"No."

He gives me a wry grin. "I should be grateful then."

I'm not sure what he means by that. I wish I could erase all those years Jimmy and I worked closely together, and I was oblivious to the depth of his delusions.

"That has nothing to do with it. You cut deals with Dolan—"

"Yeah, sure," Luca says with a dismissive gesture. "You don't need to come to me again with your self-righteous

11

shit. As if your parents never made money from those side businesses. Why do you think the Mancini Group has this much cash on hand? But you continue to live your sheltered life, princess. With that FBI woman. It's only a matter of time before you get more people killed."

"You aren't making sense, Luca. I think I better go. Take care."

"I knew you wouldn't want to hear this."

Getting to my feet, I reconsider and sit back down. "Cut the bull, Luca. If you have something to say to me, say it."

"You came here."

"I opened the doors to the FBI, and the IRS. I paid what I had to. My parents never got into drug trade. They despised the Biancos for it." I feel fairly safe saying this. I shouldn't let any doubts creep in. I can't say what his late father, my uncle Lorenzo, did, but my parents had defined lines they'd never cross. Didn't they?

"Some people are wondering how Dolan got himself killed."

I give him a shrug. "I wouldn't know. And you obviously have an alibi. Why do you care?"

"Dolan and your girl had history."

"True, but she has a federal agency behind her. She can take care of herself."

"Or you took care of it."

"Or he finally got in bed with the wrong people. You don't seem heartbroken about it either."

"Don't be ridiculous," he returns. "What I'm trying to tell you is that whatever you do, it will come back to bite you at some point. It did for your dad, right?"

That's when I know I can't get anything else out of this conversation.

"Take care of yourself. I'll come back."

"Don't bother," he mutters.

I make my way back out, pick up my belongings and go back to my car where I sit for a few minutes. He's trying to mess with me because I have everything he wanted. The business. The partner. My parents accepted me for who I am. There's no point in believing him.

I have more important things to do. Next, I call Sofia and ask her if she's free for lunch before the meeting.

"I think I can make that happen. *Catania*?"

"No. I'll pick you up."

The place I drive us to is in the vicinity of the Mancini Group, but less laden with history than *Catania*, which is important. I want neutral territory for this conversation.

Sofia, who has been quiet during the drive, doesn't seem surprised when we enter the small bistro. The hostess leads us to a private table in the back.

"I understand you had to call in the meeting so we can move forward. I just thought you'd want to get this over with quick."

"Robyn understands. She can entertain herself at home for a bit."

"She didn't know you'd offered me the job."

"It's business. I'm not obliged to disclose every single action to the FBI anymore."

"Being married doesn't make a difference? You don't have to answer that," she says when my impatience must have shown on my face. "I'm sorry. It's very generous of you, and I want to do the best job I can."

"I know you will do an excellent job. There's no big secret. I need to carve out a little time for myself, take a good look at what happened. It's poetic justice too. I'd like you to put a focus on the foundation, more than we have before." I knew that would help convincing her.

"You do a lot of good work for women in need there."

"We could do more. You have carte blanche to review any transactions."

"What will you do, Kendall? Aren't you going to get bored?"

"Aside from lending the FBI my expertise, since they asked so nicely? I will review my past and build a future."

"That sounds cryptic."

"It's not. It's just what we've always done," I say.

We take care of our own, family, even when they mess up—but especially when they didn't. Robyn always felt like family to me, but now I have a piece of paper that proves to me and the rest of the world that she is.

Chapter Three

I can't help it. I'm curious. I refuse to believe that my actions are driven by suspicion, because they're not. I've dealt with too many last-minute surprises, change of plans and danger out of nowhere.

I have to do better, for her, for myself.

Still, I can't help feeling guilty as I walk around the condo and do a thorough search. Kendall had a phone number hidden behind a painting—a number to call in case she needed to disappear. She hinted more than once that if I needed enemies out of the way, she could make it happen.

Too many times, we've barely sailed past a catastrophe. Kendall thinks she can handle it all on her own. I don't think that's the truth. I might be projecting, having a hard time getting over the night when she took a bullet to save my life.

We haven't talked about it much, not enough. I need to know what she's withholding from me, if anything.

I take a photo album out of a shelf and leaf through it, within moments engrossed in the Mancini family history. There's a photo I recognize: The great-grandparents, smiling as they stand in front of the original *Catania*, Kendall's great-grandmother holding a baby boy. Kendall's grandfather.

From there, it's both the evolution of the family and photography. There are several albums, ranging from black and white to seventies' prints with an orange tint to eighties' Polaroid and later, prints from digital cameras. I see the change in fashion, and, unmistakably, the Mancini's rise to fame and fortune.

The pictures now include the Mancini group, the Adria restaurant group, and a recurring theme, *Catania*. There's a whole album of Kendall, from day one to...I realize the happy family picture must have been one of the last with both of her parents, Alphonso and Angela. They are on a boat, toasting to one another.

I put the album aside, unsure what to feel.

She may be my wife now, and I've studied her up close, but there's still a lot I don't know. I wonder what happened to that boat.

No reason to get paranoid either—it's such a random thing. Kendall managed to get herself out of trouble by being transparent, and she'll continue to assist my unit. She has no reason to want to get away. Perhaps, deep down, it's abandonment fears that make me think one day she could, and I would be left with...What? Boredom? Regrets? She has made my life so much more exciting. And scary because I never thought I'd get this attached to anyone.

I put the albums away and continue my snooping in the kitchen. That seems safe. Fridge and pantry are full of food. There's still some champagne in the fridge, another bottle of wine. Kendall doesn't keep that much in the house, I know, because there's always *Catania*. The family restaurant means more to her than the successful, multi-billion-dollar company that is the Mancini Group. She might leave me, but she'd never leave it behind.

Where did that come from?

I inspect drawers and cabinets, an action both wrong and calming. Everything is in order, warm colors, tasteful choices. Kendall has always been comfortable with being rich, though the work she does with her foundation shows that she's aware not everyone's this fortunate. I've been wrestling with this investigation and its results. I've never wrestled with attraction—I gave in to it right away.

What did I hope to find?

There's nothing new. Kendall is organized, has a taste for décor and understated luxury. If there are skeletons in her closet, I think I have seen all of them. Jimmy Bruno. The back room of *Catania*. She's changed because it was the smart thing to do. Nothing to worry about.

~elle~

As promised, Kendall is back late in the afternoon. After a quick greeting, she heads for the shower and then gets ready to go out for dinner. I'm already dressed for this part of the day, and all I have to do is watch her.

Slipping on her dress, she gives me a knowing smile. I can't hide the truth, or the fact that I'm appreciating her body in anticipation.

We have a driver tonight. As we exit the parking garage, I'm surprised when she directs her to the Mancini Group headquarters.

"You forgot something?" I ask.

"No." Without further explanation, she walks ahead of me to the elevators, waving to the concierge on the way. We step inside, and she presses the button for the top floor.

"Okay then. Some kind of kinky fantasy you'd like to indulge in?"

She gives me a lazy smile that makes my cheeks warm—and other places. I try, but she's still better at this.

"I wasn't planning on it, but it's an idea for another day. I just wanted to show you something."

After the doors open with a soft sound, we walk along the hallway, door after door of conference rooms and offices. We arrive at hers, and Kendall opens the door to me. I step inside and look around. It's a stunning view from up here, but it's nothing new. Her desk looks clean. Shelves, filing cabinets, a sitting area by the window, nothing different.

I'm about to ask another question when she turns me to her.

"This is it," she says. "What you see is what you get."

Her kiss is both reaffirming and demanding. It's every-thing I want, though part of me wonders, does she really read my mind that well?

"I know. I investigated you for months." My words come out in a gasp as I find myself up against that desk. My questions are valid. So is desire.

She smiles, brushing her hand over my hair. "Yeah, and wasn't that fun." I can't blame her for the trace of sarcasm. "I had to come to terms with a lot of things. I agree with some, but not all of my parents' actions, the life they wanted for me, and the one I have."

"What is your conclusion?"

"You can't tell by the fact I married you? I want to do this. With you. And if you want to look at photo albums, you don't even have to ask, or sneak around to do it."

"I knew it." I'm not sure if I'm more embarrassed or irritated.

"I had those installed after we had the intruder. Sorry about that. I wanted you to come here and take a look. I had a business meeting. I'll have many more of those.

18

Monday morning, we'll go to work together. That's what it's going to be. No more hiding."

"I'm sorry."

"Don't be," she says, moving in closer. "I know you have to protect yourself, too, but not from me." Leaning in, Kendall whispers, "I'm not sorry you put that idea in my head."

"So...You want...?"

"I do, but patience is a virtue. Let's get food first."

—ele—

Kendall might be determined not to keep any more secrets from me—that doesn't mean no surprises I realize when our next destination is a high-end burger place on the 14th floor of a high rise. I'm telling myself I'm not superstitious, but I'm still relieved it's not thirteen.

"You know I'm a bit of a cliché," she says. "I could eat at *Catania* all day, every day. I thought you might want to try something different for once."

"I love *Catania*, but this is great, too." For some reason, a conversation we had about the family a while ago, springs to mind. Children running around. I might need a little more time to understand we're actually married, in it for life. It's comforting. It also raises a lot of questions we haven't addressed yet.

"I'm glad you do. It will always be there for us."

The food and craft beer are excellent. I wonder if I'll get used to this life. Kendall, even after the settlement she paid, doesn't seem to be interested in slowing down, and so I'm along for the ride. There's no chance I'll ever pay an equal share. It's something that lingers on my mind, just like Kendall's recent past—but that's not her fault. Those are issues I have to work out. Meanwhile, we are treated to another amazing meal. Monday is still far away.

The restaurant is about three quarters filled with equally well-dressed patrons, though the place is big enough to allow for privacy. Every once in a while, fragments of conversations float over to us—not enough to understand the whole context. I'm starting to relax, easing into that new, puzzling normal.

Kendall takes my hand. "This is nice," she says. It's easy for me to interpret the wistful tone. We hardly ever take a moment to slow down. That simply doesn't lend itself to our professions. We're not that kind of people which has its own downfalls. However, this, right now, is nice. It's more than that. It's perfect. Maybe it could work, the two of us, working together and building that life we always dreamed of?

Out of the corner of my eye, I see a man walking towards a table where two couples are seated. I don't know why, but I sit up straighter. Habit? Premonition?

Kendall has noticed him too. "I wonder if one of the women is his wife," she mutters. "He looks familiar."

That might not be a good thing. Then again, she does a lot of business with legit people. Could be somebody related to one of them, right?

My theory is out the window when the newcomer pulls a gun and shoots one of the men at the table point blank, and all hell breaks loose.

Chapter Four

"FBI!" Robyn yells over the cacophony of terror. "Drop your weapon!"

I know she can take care of herself, but damn, I'm experiencing a whole lot of terror, for her, for myself. The man spins around, firing again, as I reach for my own gun. Of course we came armed. My name is Mancini, and I'm married to an FBI agent—what else do you need to know?

I urge people to duck and stay down. Fortunately, most of them don't need to be prompted.

The shooter keeps firing and then runs, using a woman as shield on the way out, pushing her aside when he reaches the door. Robyn gives chase.

I get my cell phone and call my new boss, informing her about the harrowing incident still in progress.

"I'll do what I can, but we need backup quick!"

SAC Carr sounds skeptical regarding part of my assessment. "I'll send someone now, but you stay where you are, you hear me? What about the man he shot?"

I look over to where the victim is lying on the floor, unmoving. "I don't think he made it. Everyone else seems okay, considering. Look, I have to go."

"Stay where you are," she repeats tersely.

I end the call and turn off my phone, then I head for the exit. Technically, she's not the boss of me yet.

I have no intention of following orders and sitting on my hands while my wife is going after the shooter. My wife, who once survived a hostage situation, and bears the scars of it. I might have more selfish reasons as well. I don't want to be the person who waits for others to step in. I don't need to be. My training isn't just in running a billion-dollar company—I know how to hit a target as well.

"Thanks, Dad," I mutter as I head along the hallway to the stairs. It's silent out in the stairwell, and I wonder if I've been mistaken. Where did they go? To the elevators? Will he try to hide out on another floor?

Damn it. This is not how I wanted the evening to go, a kaleidoscope of nightmares surfacing all at once. I've seen this man before, but I can't place him. Is it paranoid to think it might not be a coincidence that Robyn and I were in the restaurant? I made a reservation earlier today.

But why kill the other man? Randomly? No, they seemed to know one another. I halt, unsure what to do next. Offices make up most of the real estate below, a bar and a few businesses that are closed now, at the bottom of the building. They can't have gone that far, can they?

Then I hear the sound of footsteps, and two more gunshots.

Silence.

I take off my pumps, draw my gun and make my way down the stairs. The floor below is quiet and dark. One more. The shots reverberated in the confined space, but I have a vague idea. My mind is calm and clear all of a sudden. I know what to do. Worst case scenario it could be an act of vengeance. I'm done with megalomaniac men messing with me when all I want is to enjoy an evening out with my wife.

There are rules. They have always been rules. Moving forward, I listen to the smallest sounds. I see a pair of black shoes sticking out from behind the wall and hasten my steps.

I turn the corner with my gun drawn. Robyn is pointing hers at the man. He's moaning, clutching his arm. Robyn's eyes widen when she sees me.

"It's all right. I called Rachel. They'll be here soon."

"I got it. You better put that away now," she says, a slight tremor to her voice. "Why are you here?"

"Why? What do you mean?"

I sense that the conversation isn't over, but voices and footsteps indicated that the cavalry is on the way. Robyn shakes her head before she shouts, "We're up here, 11th floor. It's under control."

I still want to ask her about her cryptic question. There's no time, because a few minutes later we are surrounded by law enforcement personnel, FBI and the local police department. Robyn directs them to the restaurant, and I find myself alone with SAC Carr.

"And it's not even your first day at work," she says. It sounds as pensive as it does sarcastic.

"I swear, it was nothing I did." Two can play that game. "All I wanted was to take my wife out to dinner on a weekend night."

"How did it look to you?" she asks.

"Not random, in any case. I didn't get a good look at the table before all hell broke loose, but the shooter walked up to them and shot the guy. That's as deliberate as I've ever seen. Robyn will confirm that."

"I'm sure she will. What part of stay where you are didn't you understand?"

I knew they were coming. Still, I bristle at her words.

"She went alone after that guy. I couldn't let that happen."

"Couldn't or wouldn't?"

When I'm about to elaborate, she holds up a hand.

"We'll deal with that later. I'll need you to come in as well. I don't believe in coincidences."

I frown as the implications sink in.

"You don't think this had anything to do with me and Robyn being there?"

"I've seen stranger things. We'll talk at the office."

"Can I go find Robyn?"

"I'd prefer you stay with me for now."

Since she's right in front of me, I can't defy her orders like before. Steeling myself for a long night, I can't allow any thought of what could have gone wrong. I couldn't always protect the people I loved. I'll never make any compromises when it comes to Robyn.

This is what she, and Rachel, will have to understand.

—ele—

They want my expertise and what's left of my connections, but of course I'm not to be in the loop about anything else. Rachel Carr takes me to a break room and tells me in no uncertain terms to stay put. Instead of having my dessert in a fancy restaurant, I get a coffee and a chocolate bar, double caramel. I don't feel like paying attention to calories or other nutritional values given the night we're having. We were supposed to be celebrating the relative freedom we'd gained. Instead...

No one has asked me about the gun yet. That in itself is strange, but I can see that everyone is preoccupied with the turn of events and trying to figure out what it means. The shooter, the victim, in the same place where we were trying to have a quiet evening.

VENGEANCE

As I sip the hot, bitter coffee, a memory springs to mind. "...walked up to him and shot him point blank."

I entered the room at that moment, interrupting the conversation my dad had with Jimmy. I remember Jimmy all but jumping to his feet to pull a chair for me. How could I not have known he was obsessed?

"Who shot whom?" I asked.

"Tom Foster is dead." Dad's tone was somber, and Jimmy sobered up as well. "We're trying to figure out what happened." We, meaning him, Jimmy and the third man in the room.

I'd completely forgotten about this, because soon after, my father went to a fundraiser that ended in a shootout, and him dead as well.

Tom Foster, a wealthy businessman, someone dad had lunches with on occasion, killed in the same manner as the man in the restaurant. That wasn't the only thing that bothered me though. Why was Frank Bianco there? His father had declared all of us sworn enemies after Sofia found shelter with my parents. Frank was an abuser. I didn't learn until recently that Jimmy had put himself up for hire for the Biancos, but why would Dad let Frank into his home?

It makes no sense. I get another coffee, and finish the overly sweet chocolate bar, finding no satisfaction and no answers. When the door opens, I hope it's Robyn who tells me we can go home, or finish up here with Rachel, or...something. I am disappointed. It's her partner Hampton McKay walking in.

"Ms. Mancini," he says. "What a turbulent start to you working with us." I detect various nuances in his tone, and I have no patience for either of them. He's a bit jealous, I assume—not in a sexual way, because he must have known for a long time that Robyn is a lesbian. It's more that he doesn't seem to think I deserve everything

25

I have, my wealth, my freedom, this new assignment, and also Robyn's time and attention.

"Turbulent? That's a euphemism. A man was shot and killed in front of me."

"Not for the first time, I assume."

"That's harsh. I was hoping that your impression of me would be more rooted in reality, and less in a Hollywood movie."

He smiles wryly. "Don't worry, I think my impression is accurate."

"My father didn't shoot people for the heck of it, and neither did I."

"I believe that. Usually, it would be Jimmy Bruno who got his hands dirty. You wouldn't be in the room."

He's not completely wrong.

"What are you getting at?" I ask. "I didn't need to be here. I agreed to help where I can, and right now I'm waiting for my wife. I'm not being detained, and I sure as hell won't be interrogated."

"Relax, no one's interrogating you. Just making conversation."

"I'm surprised you can find the time when everyone else is busy but suit yourself. You might want to look into the case of Tom Foster. My father talked about this once. Businessman, was killed in the same manner if I remember correctly."

"You remembered that just now?" he asks.

I don't roll my eyes at him, but I want to.

"Agent McKay, I paid more to the IRS than you will ever earn in your entire career. If you could give me a break?" That was probably unnecessary, but I couldn't help myself. "It came back to me now, yes. Think what you want about me. I just though this connection might be of interest to you."

He gets up to get a coffee for himself. "It is. You must know we appreciate your help."

"Sure."

"It's interesting that those connections you're talking about...They all lead to you, once again."

"What can I say? I'm not nobody. You think after the year I've had—years, actually—you can scare me with anything? I'm more than willing to help where I can, but I need you to do your job."

"That's why we're here. See you later, Ms. Mancini."

"Wait!" I call after him when he turns and leaves. "When can I see Robyn?"

"SAC Carr expressed herself clearly, didn't she? Wait here. Robyn will find you when she's done."

More mediocre coffee and too much sugar it is.

What the hell is wrong with him? It might be that I'm easily alarmed after a long-time trustee of my dad's turned out to be his murderer, and my cousin ran a drug ring out of the restaurant group—but something irks me about McKay. I'll have to talk to Robyn about this. She of all people knows I'm not paranoid.

—— *elle* ——

Robyn is tight-lipped when she comes to get me later that night. Even with all the caffeine and sugar I was about to nod off. I tried her phone a few times to no avail.

"You have no idea how happy I am to see you," I say as I get to my feet. "The selection in here could be better."

"Let's go home."

"What did you find out about the guy?"

"Later. I just want to get out of here."

"Of course."

In the car, I try again. "So, is there anything you can tell me?"

Robyn shrugs. "It's late. Give it a few hours, okay?"

"You're still mad at me?"

"For Christ's sake, Kendall, not everything is about you!" she explodes, and that shuts me up for a while. I hang on to my own thoughts. I know that she's been under a lot of pressure, has been since the day she started researching me. Kendall Mancini, the big career changing assignment. Only things didn't go quite as planned. She was ready to cross lines to make me trust her.

Neither of us expected that we would get married, drawn to each other in a way neither of us was able to resist.

That hasn't changed.

When we are at the condo, I announce that I'll take a quick shower.

"Perhaps we could have a snack afterwards?"

Robyn tries to hide the smile, but I've seen it.

"You're still hungry?"

"We never had a real dessert. And it's closer to breakfast now, so yes, I am."

I'm hopeful that she might be willing to forgive me for my earlier transgressions. I might have a chance. I've barely stepped under the shower spray when she opens the stall and steps inside with me, urgency in her gaze.

Seconds later, I yelp as my back makes contact with the cold tile. She kisses me, hard, her hands roaming my body possessively, soon eliciting a different kind of sounds. I guess that conversation, and snack, can wait.

Chapter Five

"**W**hat the hell is wrong with you?"

Kendall's jaw drops a bit, and perhaps for a reason. It's not what a woman wants to hear after quick, but amazing sex. I've been running on adrenaline all day, for many days, and I'm starting to crash. We put on robes after the water turned cold, but I feel like I can't get warm.

"There I thought we handled everything well enough, given the circumstances. I'm sorry the man is dead. He never had a chance, but you caught his killer."

She wasn't wrong earlier. I am hungry, too, and I didn't have nearly enough wine at the restaurant. I might be trying to fill a different kind of need, with sex, food, and alcohol. It doesn't matter. Right now, all of it is what I need.

"More people could have been killed. There could have been a second shooter. Rachel told you to stay put. I had it covered!"

"I know you did. I was worried about you."

Kendall is telling me this as if I have no point whatso-ever, as if her actions were completely normal.

"You always bring a gun to a restaurant?" I ask.

"Habit," she says with a shrug. "No one told me I couldn't. I have the paperwork for it, and frankly I don't regret it."

I take a deep breath, still feeling shaky in a way that cheese, grapes, and nuts might not help with. With a sip of the red wine—now that's better.

"I haven't told anyone. I'd prefer if you leave it at home from now on."

"I don't want to lie to you, so could we postpone that subject until tomorrow?"

How can she be so casual about this? I do know the answer though. Kendall has gotten away with a lot in her life. There have been too many close calls lately.

"Tobias Wilder. The name ring any bell to you?"

"No, should it?" The surprise is genuine. I am sure she is telling the truth, which hasn't always been the case.

"He's in Financial Services. We don't know much more about him, but we're still looking. No red flags so far." I am also sure that they will turn up eventually. This was no random killing. "Hampton told me what you said to him."

"You're looking into the Foster case, right? Same M.O."

"Foster was a competitor of your dad's?"

"I don't know that I'd call it that. They often had lunch together. I don't remember him that much beyond those lunches, but Dad sure wanted to know who killed him."

"Was he worried it might come back to him?"

"He was worried because the guy was dead. He had a conversation about it with Jimmy...and Frank Bianco."

I sit down at the table, stalling the inevitable. I take another sip of wine first.

"Frank Bianco. And you didn't think that was a detail that could have been helpful?" I am deeply, hopelessly in love with this woman. The fact that she risked her life tonight still fills me with dread, but I swear, sometimes I don't understand her at all. This is one of those moments.

"I was going to tell you, but you weren't there, and when you came to get me, you didn't want to talk."

"What was he doing there? I thought that the Biancos hated your parents because they took in Sofia."

"I don't know what to tell you. It baffled me too. I don't think I ever saw him at the house again."

"What about Jimmy?"

"Yes, what about Jimmy? Now I keep wondering if he knew more about the issue. Maybe bringing Frank there was his idea."

"All right. Why didn't you tell Hampton?"

Kendall's expression becomes guarded, and I'm certain the answer is something I don't want to hear—though I couldn't imagine what that would be. Hampton's reputation is beyond reproach. He's one of the good guys.

"Come on."

She makes me wait, filling her plate, then her glass of wine before she speaks.

"You know him better than I do."

"I know him quite well, yes. He has a stellar record, and he's a good friend."

"At some point, I thought I could rely on Jimmy."

"This is ridiculous! You're not comparing Hampton to the guy who did the dirty work for your family?"

She knows that she's gone too far. Her expression is somewhere between apologetic and pained.

"No, I'm not, not really. Perhaps I'm a bit sensitive where the subject is concerned. He doesn't like me," she adds with a shrug. "I guess he has his reasons that have nothing to do with the case."

"He has a wife. He was never interested in me in that way." Even as I say it, I'm reminded of Jimmy Bruno's obsession with Kendall that led him to murder her father. There is no comparison. There's a world between Hampton and men like Bruno. "Why are we even talking about this? You had any good reason to withhold that detail about Frank Bianco—other than Hampton being a jerk to you? If he was, I'll handle it, but you know this could be important."

"I know. Now that it came back to me, I can't help wondering why Dad would even let him in. For most of my life, I was taught not to respect any Bianco because they all covered for Frank when he abused Sofia. Damn it. Is everyone leaving me riddles to figure out from the grave now?"

She sounds genuinely distressed. I can forgive her for questioning my partner of five years. To be honest, even good men can get queasy when confronted with a woman in power. I never pegged Hampton to be one of those, but Kendall Mancini, my wife, is definitely a special case.

"Maybe it's not such a riddle. There are still people around we can ask."

"I wish we could stop bothering Sofia at some point. Frank isn't going to talk."

"I didn't mean Sofia," I say. "I have an idea." Checking my watch, I realize Hampton and Rachel are probably asleep. This will have to wait a few hours, which isn't a bad thing.

"I guess that means no sleep?"

"We have wine and food. The rest, I'll make it up to you."

A smile is playing over her lips, and for a moment, it would be easy to forget all about duty and the riddle to solve.

"I thought you already did," she says.

I get mad at her. I get frustrated. It's probably mutual, but none of it matters. I am where I'm supposed to be, doing the job I was meant to do, being with her. Even if the two interact in complicated ways.

Hampton is unimpressed when I bring the additional detail to him early the next morning. We have breakfast together before we go in. I can't believe I'm hungry again, but between trying to answer burning questions, and an equally burning desire, I spent a lot of energy...

He doesn't need to know any of this—and he doesn't want to, I'm sure. Kendall isn't naïve, but the thought that he might be jealous seems outlandish to me. I came out to him years ago, and he never even blinked.

"You don't think the fact that Bianco was there is of any importance?" I say before biting into a muffin.

"You think it is? We've looked into Tom Foster. There are some similarities, but not enough to establish a pattern. We don't even know enough about the shooter yet. Two different men, different weapons."

"Same M.O."

"Something Ms. Mancini conveniently remembered. What if she's trying to divert attention from herself?" He shakes his head. "I know you're a risk taker, but I still can't wrap my head around the fact that you married her. This is wrong on so many levels."

I'm confused, and a little offended. "She did everything she was supposed to. Rachel hired her as a consultant. I'm not sure what you're trying to tell me."

Hampton studies me as if I'm the one who's not getting it. I'm beginning to get impatient with his approach. I can't have Kendall's theory be true, not even a little part of it. My life is complicated enough as it is.

"Claudia and Luca are taking the fall for the mess that happened at Adria, now that it's sold, and Kendall has a solid business on her hands with the Mancini Group. Add to that *Catania*. As usual, she comes out on top. Are you sure that's all there is?"

"I am. She cooperated, helped us dismantle the drug ring out of Adria, and paid the money she owed to the government."

"Yeah, she reminded me of that too. I'd be surprised though if it was all clean now."

"That's cynical. You don't have to like her, but you can acknowledge that people can change."

"Do they? Someone doing business of that kind, on that scale?" He looks doubtful.

I realize my muffin is gone, and I reach for another one from the basket. Stress doesn't hinder my appetite. On the contrary.

"We have to check in with the detective who's on last night's murder," I say. "I think it's the more pressing issue. Unless you have proof that Kendall is withholding something." It's a gamble, and for a few seconds I worry that he might actually come up with something. That is not the case. "So that's it. You don't have to be friends. I've come to know her. All she ever wanted was to protect the people she cares about."

"That and move every obstacle out of the way while still living the luxury life."

"What the hell is this? You think I don't deserve any of it?"

"That's not what I said, and you know it. You used to have a different take on all of this too. You changed, Robyn. She changed you."

At this point, I wish there was a third muffin in the basket.

"I'll have to call the detective now and see where they are. I have another appointment later."

"You know it's true."

The waitress comes by to refill our coffees, and I eagerly push my cup towards her.

"Thank you so much."

I'm going to need every last drop of it.

Before I get on my way, I check in with Rachel, and the detective on the murder case, a woman Ashley Carter. She confirms that they are following several leads. The man I apprehended hasn't talked yet. I'll get a shot at him later. My own thought makes me wince.

During the drive, I keep the radio cranked up on Classic Rock. I am not ready to analyze the conversation I had with Hampton, and where it turned a tad heated, so I think about Tom Foster.

His business still exists, run by his life partner of thirty-five years. There are no obvious ties to organized crime save for the lunches Tom used to have with Alphonso Mancini. Both of them dead.

The man serving a life sentence for Mancini's murder should have some answers for me. Given the fact that he abducted and beat me not long ago, I'll take immense satisfaction from seeing him behind bars.

I know Kendall went to see her cousin Luca in prison. Their relationship is complicated. She gave him up because of his involvement in the drug ring. It's much clearer between me and Jimmy Bruno. Law enforcement. Murderer. If anyone's jealous of me, it's him. He always wanted Kendall, regardless of the fact that she was out and dating women.

He looks surprised to see me. Perhaps he hoped that she would come to visit him.

"Hey, Jimmy," I say.

He stares back at me wordlessly. No need for pretense. He hates me. He thought he was doing Kendall a favor when he wanted to make me disappear, for her. She didn't see it the same way.

We are both silent for what feels like an eternity. But I'm used to it. He cracks first.

"What do want from me?"

"Just talk."

"What if I don't want to?"

"You're here. That tells me you're either curious or bored enough. Tell me about Tom Foster."

He gives me an incredulous laugh.

"Really? You came here to get my help with an old murder case? I might be bored, but you're desperate, Agent Johnson."

He loved to sneer in my face basically from the moment we met. Nothing much has changed, I see.

"I see you're not going to talk." Between the two of us, he is clearly the more desperate one. All it takes for me is to touch my wedding ring, turn it on my finger. The flash of fury on his face is quite spectacular. He's struggling to keep his composure—still pining for Kendall.

"You might have forgotten for a moment who's in charge here. That's right, Jimmy, not you. They locked you up in here and threw away the key. Oh well. You do what you want." I get to my feet. "I thought you might get a kick out of the fact that someone was actually interested in your opinion. I see it's not the case."

"My opinion about what?" he asks, irritated. "Foster was shot in a restaurant. Guy walked up to him and pulled the trigger."

"You discussed this with Alphonso." I remain standing.

"He had him over a few times. They worked on a project together. Al was worried people might put two and two together."

I have to be careful. For almost two decades, Jimmy was privy to lots of Alphonso's secrets, though he had his own agenda for most of that time. Get to Kendall. Get access to the Mancini's immense fortune.

"Why would anyone suspect him? And why did you two discuss this with Frank Bianco?"

His eyes widen slightly, and I know I'm on to something.

"That was your idea, wasn't it? Bringing in Frank?"

"You've been talking to him? What did he tell you?"

I shake my head with a wry smile.

"No, it doesn't work that way. If you have an idea, I'd like to hear it. Otherwise, I'm out of here."

"I can tell you Frank wouldn't be too happy about me sharing my ideas with you, so I won't. He still has friends on the inside."

"You and Frank killed him together? To make Alphonso look bad?"

"No, it wasn't like that at all."

"I'm surprised you managed to convince Alphonso to let Frank Bianco into his house. I guess he never had any idea what you were up to."

"You're wrong," he mutters. "This didn't have anything to do with me, or Sofia, if that's what you mean. You're wasting your time, Agent Johnson. Go home."

"I'm starting to think you're right. But Kendall was right too. She said you had a big mouth, but you weren't all that."

The flash of anger is predictable, still impressive. I don't shrink back.

"She might respect you if you did the right thing for once, but I don't see that happening."

I'm running out of ways to appeal to this man's ego. Kendall has no respect for him and never will—he murdered her father. I hope he's self-righteous enough to fall for it anyway.

"You're lying," he spits. "Kendall got distracted and confused, otherwise she'd know the right thing would have been for us to take care of business, and the family.

37

Alphonso indulged her. This is why I needed him to get out of the way."

He's getting off path a bit, but I still have faith.

"He was far too soft. Hanging with Foster, letting Kendall have those silly affairs when he knew she and I could do great things together. He didn't need to die." I'm shocked to realize he's close to tears.

"And Tom Foster? Did he need to die?"

"I don't know who killed him if that's what you mean. Frank came to warn us about another player in town."

"Arturo Rossi?"

He scoffs. "Rossi has always been a nobody. No, someone with more influence and capital. Someone who might have shaken things up."

"You have a name?"

"No. He didn't have a lot of information though he believed that this third party could be dangerous to the stability we'd established. Then Kendall walked in, and the conversation ended. Frank left and I never saw him at the house again."

"You saw him a few other times when you two planned Alphonso's murder."

He doesn't deny or confirm.

I guess I have something I can bring home to Kendall now.

First, I have to meet the killer we arrested yesterday.

Chapter Six

I'll meet with Carr and the other agents later in the day. I guess they'll try and keep me away from Robyn to some extent, which makes sense. We need to protect her and protect the process. I understand these measures very well, because we've been taking them for our family, Mom and Dad before me.

My mind is still reeling with all the implications, Dad inviting Frank Bianco to discuss matters of Tom Foster's death—not to mention the fact that we brought down an armed shooter. Well, Robyn did. I'm curious to see what she'll learn today.

I still have time to take care of my own business for a few hours first and meet Sofia.

When she comes into my office where I had the kitchen prepare coffee and a snack, I can't help thinking that she's changed. She started to work for the company shortly after my parents took her in, launched a career from there. As long as I remember, she's been a steady but quiet presence.

She holds herself with a new confidence. I'm glad I trusted her, and I'm convinced I made the right choice. She and the women who benefit from the foundation deserve better than living with a petty, small-minded abuser. Which brings me back to the burning questions.

"You're well stocked as always," she remarks with regard to the delicacies on the table.

"What can I say? I've given this business many hours. I can't do it without a good amount of food. I just wanted to hear how things are going."

Her stance becomes wary.

"If they weren't going well, you would have heard by now, so what are you really asking?"

You can't fool someone who has lived through the experiences she had.

"Sorry about that. I swear I'll get to it. Do you remember anything about Tom Foster's murder?"

"Of course," she says, sounding surprised. "Don't you? I mean you were younger. For a while they thought it might be a hate crime. Tony Bianco made a lot of noise about the new player and how your dad should do business with him again if he wanted to prevail. A lot of blustering."

"You think Tony and Frank made up that new player? To convince Dad?"

"They might, but your father wasn't a fool. I don't think he would have fallen for it."

What does it say about me that I'm not certain while she is? Maybe it's still the hardest to accept that I made the same mistakes with Jimmy as he had. Jimmy was just always around. Doing the job that was asked of him, and he was well reimbursed. I never thought...

"Would they want to set him up?"

"You should ask them. Frank that is." I swear saying his name made her flinch. I don't want to go there, but I think I have to.

"Dad had Jimmy and Frank over to discuss what happened with Foster. Now I think this is related to their theory, or ruse, about that third player. What if they wanted to frame Dad, it didn't work, and *then* they decided to kill him?"

40

"It's a possibility," Sofia agrees. She bursts my bubble seconds later. "I'm not sure what you thought, but none of this is particularly new to me. Like I said, there was always bluster, but behind closed doors, Al and Tony needed each other in some twisted way. For the *equilibrium*, that part wasn't so wrong. It told others to stay out, that it was taken care off. There were background deals."

I make a frustrated sound. "Basically, I knew nothing when I took over."

"Oh, that's not entirely true. You know your stuff, how to run the company. The finer details...Well, you don't have to worry about that anymore, I guess. For the record, I don't blame Al. He promised me I'd be safe, that I'd have work and a roof over my head, and he always kept that promise. You made me CEO. Everything else is no longer our problem."

"Except that a man was shot in a place where Robyn and I were having dinner. Same style as Foster. I'd say that is a problem."

She shrugs. "It's something for the police department and the FBI to figure out, no? I thought they wanted you to consult on certain cases, not do investigative work full-time."

If she sounds a tad impatient, perhaps I deserve it.

"I see your point, I swear. I want to make sure I didn't miss anything, that Foster wasn't a sign of things to come."

I'm still not sure. Why that man, why this specific restaurant?

"If it was, someone waited a long time to have it all unfold." Sofia pauses, an uncomfortable silence ensuing before she voices what we both know. "Then again, it's not unheard of."

The long game, building up to vengeance. But to what end?

41

"What I'm trying to tell you is that whatever you do, it will come back to bite you at some point. Sadly, it did for your dad, even though he had the best of intentions. You have to be careful, Kendall."

Luca's cryptic words come back to me, and the memory makes me wonder if he had something specific in mind, or if he was just messing with me.

It would be a big coincidence. I didn't mention it to Robyn, and she might think I'm trying to keep something from her.

Is there a third player?

Is Frank Bianco trying to pull strings from behind bars?

"I will be. I promise," I add when she raises an eyebrow. "But we'll have to get to the bottom of this. People will need to understand that things have changed. The equilibrium is a different one now. I won't have these things happen in my city."

That elicits a wry smile from Sofia like I knew it would. What can I say? We are all prone to drama. It doesn't mean we're not serious. I have a lot of people watching me, and they all need to understand I mean business.

End of story.

Chapter Seven

The shooter is still in the hospital, cuffs tying one wrist to the hospital bed.

He gives me and the detective an angry stare. She and I exchange a wry smile. We didn't expect anything else.

"I have nothing to tell you," he starts.

I let Detective Carter take the lead, observe.

"That's all right, Mr. Peck. We'll talk instead. It's an interesting résumé you have. You worked for Tom Foster for three years, then you were on the Adria group's payroll. Nothing for a while, then all of a sudden, you emerge, walk up to a businessman and shoot him. Same way Foster died. That would be a huge coincidence, wouldn't you say?"

He doesn't say anything, which is just as well. The pieces of the puzzle come together, revealing more connections to the Mancinis. I suppress a sigh. This makes it even less likely the shooter—and whoever hired him—didn't already know that Kendall and I would be there.

"Suit yourself. My colleagues are going through your electronic devices right now. I assume we don't need you to actually say it, but what we've found is already interesting."

"You didn't find shit," he spits.

"The encryption was a challenge, I'll admit it. But we've had excellent resources thanks to our friends at the FBI, and we already knew what to look for. So, no, you don't need to say it. Your phone records are a thing of beauty when it comes to evidence."

He is beet red, beads of sweat forming on his forehead.

"You're bluffing."

"I could be," she says. "Agent Johnson will explain to you why we're not."

I step forward. "*Capo dei capi*. We'll find out anyway who's behind that name, but if you tell us now, you'll save us a lot of time, and you might have some time on the outside left."

He laughs in my face as if I said something amusing.

"You're ready to spend the rest of your life in prison for that man. I guess there's nothing much we can do here."

"You brushed up on your vocabulary?" He snickers. "*Goomar.*"

I'm caught off guard for a second, though I should have expected this to come up at some point. Kendall's family, cousins Luca and Claudia and their late father Lorenzo were fairly mum on the subject, because they all had their own skeletons in their respective closets. This man doesn't have much to lose, which he is demonstrating to me by calling me a term used for the mistress of a mafia boss.

I catch the quick, curious look the detective gives me.

"I see what you'd like to imply, but whoever told you, wasn't up to date. I'm no one's mistress, and this isn't about Kendall. I wouldn't be here if it was."

"You know nothing," he sneers. "Everything is always about the princess."

This is not what I wanted to hear.

"This is bullshit. She had no ties to Foster, her father did. No ties to the man you killed. Someone's trying to tell a different story, let's say, your boss, they must have a lot to lose—or are trying out for petty revenge. You called the penitentiary, five times. You know we can check the logs, and who you talked to."

"Bruno, Bianco, sure." He snorts.

"Is one of them trying to stage a comeback?"

"They're amateurs. Nobody I'd be proud to work with."

"Interesting." And somewhat reassuring. It would be one of the worst-case scenarios to have Jimmy Bruno, or Frank Bianco, on the run.

"I have nothing more to say to you. Talk to my lawyer."

I'm not sure if he's simply not that smart, because he told us a lot already.

"Want to grab a coffee on the way?" the detective asks when we walk along the hallway of the hospital. I never say no to caffeine, and it's a good idea to get some and brainstorm based on this information.

I'm in for a surprise.

"Mind if I join you?"

I turn around to face Kendall.

"I might have some things to add to that conversation," she says, not before giving the detective the once over. I'm not sure if Rachel sent her, or if Kendall decided she was going to check on that cooperative work with the female detective.

Ashley Carter extends her hand to Kendall. "Ms. Mancini, of course. I'm interested in hearing your perspective."

I almost roll my eyes. Why is it that I had to prepare months for my undercover assignment when everyone around me is just opening doors to her? Kendall gives me a triumphant smile.

"Me too," I say. "All right. Let's get coffee."

45

There's melancholy in Kendall's expression when I repeat the term to her. "*Capo dei capi*? That used to be Dad no matter how much Tony wanted a piece of it."

I don't want to rain on her parade, though I doubt that many of the lesser crime lords saw it that way. Alphonso stayed away from the drug trade, and he tried to curb the violence. Worked with the FBI. I'm not sure how well that went over with some of his associates, his murder case in point. Jimmy Bruno wanted the Mancini Group as much as he wanted Kendall, and he wasn't above killing.

"You think someone's taking the title? The famous third player lying in wait?" The detective sounds interested but wary. I know there's another interpretation, and it's not good.

Kendall catches it. "It's not me, in any case, if that's what you were asking. I'm doing everything by the letter of the law, with the real estate group, and the family restaurant. I think Robyn here can attest to that, but so can the entire unit. You must know what happened at Adria. Those restaurants no longer belong to me."

"And you made Sofia Bianco CEO of the company."

"You did your homework."

The detective gives her a wry smile. "I think your wife can attest to that...everyone working in law enforcement in this city does their homework. It makes life easier. Don't worry, it's obvious you're running a clean business now. So did Tom Foster."

"Ouch."

"Yes. SAC Carr assured me we'll have access to all the resources we need. So, that includes you, Ms. Mancini. I wasn't just polite when I said I was interested in your opinion. So, who do you think is the famous boss of bosses?"

Kendall gives this some thought.

"I've been wondering about that. Given where this came from, the Biancos, and Jimmy, I'm tempted to believe he never existed. It might have been a ploy to begin with. They were setting up my father. They might have started there, trying to talk Dad into something..." She breaks off, frustrated. "I wish I knew more details, but I've been hitting walls for some time. Strange they all have to do with Jimmy and Frank. I'm not sure how much of it played into their motivation, but on top of hating my family for helping Sofia, homophobia might have been part of it. So, no, I wouldn't look at a possible third player. I'd look at the Biancos again."

"Thanks to you, the authorities have for the past few months, and there was a lot to find."

"There sure was," I agree, realizing that there was a bit of sarcasm to the detective's comment. "You haven't seen all the paperwork, I assume."

"It wasn't getting married to the agent that allowed me to keep my business," Kendall adds. "If there was a lot to find it's because I gave Robyn and her colleagues everything I had, and I had to make some painful decisions in the process."

A stand-off is not helpful, at this time, or any time.

"So, what do you say? Back to Frank?" the detective asks.

She shrugs. "I'm not sure what leverage you could have. If you let him out, he's going to kill me."

A chilling prospect. There's one thing I can assure her of, though.

"He's not going to get out," I promise. "We'll start smaller and take a look at everyone who's been around him lately. Then we cross-reference with known associates around the time of Foster's murder."

"Sounds like a plan," Detective Carter agrees. "You'll keep in touch?"

"Definitely." I don't want either one to know how freaked out I am at the possibilities, no matter now small.

Chapter Eight

We dine at *Catania* tonight. After the unexpected events, the comfort and familiarity are most welcome. No matter what happens. This was the vision of my great-grandparents, that no matter how much success or loss our family would face, this place would always be ours, an escape from the world.

This still rings true, and it's somewhat ironic that it's more comforting being here than thinking of the ultimate plan B. Or Z, I'm not sure where we'll be once, and if, I have to implement it.

Robyn infiltrated the company as an unpaid intern of sorts. Now we're basically colleagues again, but I'm on her turf. Did we achieve something better? Did we make the world safer? There are still too many men out there who kill at the drop of a hat. The shooter.

Frank Bianco—I wasn't kidding when I said he'll come for me the moment he has the chance.

Dark thoughts on an otherwise lovely evening.

Robyn investigated me. She fell for me. She married me. That's kind of wondrous.

I study her as she sits across from me, wearing a casual dress, her hair in a ponytail.

"What?" she asks, predictably picking up on the scrutiny.

"You're beautiful," I say, and she smiles, the last trace of fatigue from a long day vanishing.

"I've seen better days but thank you."

"I mean it. I'm aware I'm not the only one who has given up something."

Her career likely isn't on the same trajectory it was when she took on my case.

"I'm not sure I want to get into that tonight," she says. "I'm still wondering if we overlooked something. I mean...Frank was always on our radar, and so was Jimmy, early on. I'm not sure either one knows much. They're cocky, tease with information...but maybe they're just bored and trying to get a rise out of us."

There was a time when I thought I could rely on Jimmy. That is now tinged with shame. I loved both of my parents dearly, but I wish they'd shown better judgement where he was concerned. Not that I can blame them for all of it. I showed the same bad judgement.

"I wouldn't put it past either of them."

She's right though, something still doesn't add up. My "expertise" isn't helping much.

"Another thing. I'm not even sure if it's that important, but the timing is curious. When I saw Luca, he hinted at things to come."

Robyn sits up straighter.

"What does that mean? He threatened you? Why didn't you tell me?"

I hold up a hand. "I am telling you now. It was subtle, but with all that talk going around and the shooting...I just don't know."

"You think he's somehow in touch with Bianco or Bruno?"

It's a tough question. "He lost his father too because of the Biancos. There's no love lost there. But he did team up with Jimmy before...I'm sorry," I say when I see her flinch. Not the best of memories for either one of us, more painful for her.

"It's okay. I see where you're going, but Luca was worried about his dad finding out he's gay, right? With Lorenzo gone, he didn't have any more ties to Jimmy—and his dealings at Adria were unrelated." She sighs, her frustration obvious. "What the hell are they up to?"

"I'll ask around. My extended family might be wary, but they understand that I had their back when delivering the Biancos. Jimmy and Luca both became liabilities when they strayed from the path so to speak."

"You think some of your cousins still like you?" A wry smile plays over her lips.

"I'll find out. I'll get back to you with everything I find right away," I promise.

"You better," Robyn reminds me and steals a piece of pizza off my plate. "What? It's your fault for introducing me to this place. This is still the best I've ever had."

"And you thought I was exaggerating when I told you the first time."

She holds my gaze. "I've been carefully vetting everything you told me. This is why we're here."

I sense that shop talk is over. I'm good with that, flagging the waiter to refill our glasses.

It's late when we return home, and given the task ahead, we make it an early night. Sleep doesn't come easily. If Frank is after me, it's a valid question to ask why he didn't send the shooter straight to me. The person behind this, did they mean to send a warning, that they're going to move closer with each hit? Tom Foster died, and then my dad. The man at the restaurant—am I next on the list? Or does someone want to make me look bad? When my parents, and Uncle Lorenzo, were still alive, we used to have regular family dinners, sometimes at *Catania*, sometimes in individual homes.

We've let it lapse lately. Lorenzo's death, Luca's arrest, a lot has happened and perhaps some of my remaining family isn't so sure where they stand, or where we stand. Time to remind them. Talking to Claudia is always a good start to gauge the temperature.

"Can't sleep?" Robyn asks wearily.

"Is it that obvious? I'm sorry I woke you."

"You didn't. I keep thinking about this too. Maybe we aren't seeing the forest for the trees."

I turn to her.

"What's not to see? The Biancos, Jimmy. They might be behind bars, but they still have some loyalists on the outside. Lorenzo even gave me a speech once about how people sympathize with Jimmy because of his un-requited love for me." I shake my head remembering that conversation. It was disheartening. Lorenzo pretty much had a free ride at the Adria group, and still he supported the attitudes of people hostile to our family. People that eventually got him killed. "It makes no sense. The third player doesn't. I can see some sympathizing with Jimmy, still, but he's not important enough. Frank Bianco might be if he wanted to start over, but most of the infrastructure is gone. Whoever is out there still supporting him would be smart to lay low, not order or execute a hit."

"What if they want to show how bold they are? That they can take you on?"

"I'm a Mancini, married to an FBI agent." I say this with pride. All of it. "They must know they're asking for trouble."

She's on top of me, kissing me deeply the next moment. I have to admit I didn't expect it, but I'm more than happy to go with the suggestion.

"What's that for?" The words come out in a blissful gasp.

"I hate that we'll always have this hanging over us, some nemesis or another trying to get a piece of the cake. But what you said, it's also pretty...hot."

"I can show you hot."

"Please do," she whispers.

I aim to please, though I can't help thinking she hit a nerve. We're both tired—but I don't know a life in which no one wants to take power away from me. Let them try.

Chapter Nine

"This is not protocol," I state, and Kendall starts laughing. I deserved that, but still.

"I don't think multiple orgasms were ever in the protocol," she says, looking pleased with herself even after I nearly choke on my bite of donut.

I am sitting in a parked car with my wife, the ride-along consultant. It's lucky no one else can hear her frank assessment of the situation. We are in front of the new offices Claudia rented after the sale of Adria. Her part is still related to the restaurant business even after her botched deal with Arturo Rossi. Kendall thought talking to her might be worthwhile. She suggested keeping it low-key.

Low-key is fine with me. Claudia has all sorts of troubling connections, one of them the short affair with Frank Bianco. Somehow, she always came out fairly unscathed. I have a feeling there's still a lot to uncover.

"She's my cousin. I think she's over being pissed at me now, so I'll just go in, ask a few questions and that will be it."

It's never that easy, I think. Claudia has told me before, without reservation, that she'd be ready to take over because Kendall, in Claudia's words, made "too many mistakes."

"Be careful."

"You're worried about me?" she asks with a smug smile, and I barely refrain from rolling my eyes at her.

"You have given me plenty of reasons."

"Ouch. Okay. I'll see you in a bit."

I tell myself that consolidation is a good thing. Maybe Claudia will understand that Kendall isn't the enemy, hell, not even the FBI is the enemy. It's the attitude of people like the Biancos, and even some men in the Mancini family that have held the women back.

Well, as much as anyone can hold Kendall back, because she won't have any of it. If push comes to shove, Claudia is better off working with her cousin. They can protect each other, so I can do my job protecting the city. Easy in theory.

Kendall comes back out of the building sooner than I expected, her expression pensive and worried.

I reach over to open the door for her.

"How did it go?"

"Okay, I guess. No bad surprises which is improvement."

"But?" I prompt.

She sits inside and fastens her seatbelt. "She's playing it cool as usual, but this is something new. I think she's scared."

"Why? Of whom?"

"Of random people walking up to her in public and shooting her? She denied that there's anything to worry about, and she agreed with me that there is no third player."

I let that sink in for a moment. The question is still hanging in the air.

"Her affair with Frank was a while ago. She hasn't been privy to any Bianco secrets in some time, not that I think he ever shared much with her." Kendall shakes her head. "I still don't get it, but that's her life. I just don't see the connection."

"It's probably not something she's proud of now, so I can understand why she wouldn't go into details."

"There you have it," Kendall says with a sigh. "I don't need to consult you or your boss on that. People make mistakes, especially when it comes to sex."

That is a loaded statement. I know she's talking about Claudia who had an affair with the Bianco son whose abusive behavior had much to do with the family rivalry. Or perhaps she includes Cousin Luca who's still married to his wife Elena but had relationships with men on the side. One in particular? I tell myself to put a pin in that. Tom Foster, too, was gay. It might be a reach, but I have to look at this from all angles.

"Just for the record, I didn't mean us. The house of cards was going to come down one way or another. I have to say I could understand your motivation better than Jimmy's, Luca's or Claudia's. You were supposed to work against me. They weren't."

Maybe I had hoped she wouldn't still see it that way, but that would be naïve.

"Will you ever forgive me?" I'm only half joking.

"Oh, I forgave you a long time ago," she says. "Claudia and Luca, I'm not there yet. They are still pretty self-righteous given everything they did behind my back. Jimmy, of course, is done."

"How did you end it with Claudia?"

"The way you and I discussed. She'll get back to me if she finds anything. So, you think I could go back to my day job?"

"Actually, I'd like you to come to the office with me. I'd like to run some ideas by you."

Kendall looks intrigued. "It's not like I can say no, but this sounds interesting."

"I'm glad, because actually, yes, you could say no. You're a consultant, not a suspect."

She gives me a long look.

"I'm still not sure if it makes a big difference."

Kendall isn't entirely wrong. Rachel didn't advocate for having her come on board out of the goodness of her heart. Kendall isn't an enemy to the FBI. It would be too soon to call her a friend, but either way, we are keeping her close.

I'll admit it's not the worst feeling to have that kind of power, because she has a lot over me.

—ele—

Hampton looks surprised and not too pleased when Kendall and I step into the room where the board is already set up for the case.

Peck. His victim, Tobias Wilder. His connections to Adria and Tom Foster. Luca and Claudia. But we're aware of the secrets the latter kept—all of them?

"You need me for this?" he asks. "I have a meeting in ten."

"I can fill you in later." I swear he scowls at that before he leaves. Kendall watches him walk away, a hint of amusement in her expression. I have no use for this, especially not here.

"Okay, Bruno. I know you revoked access to accounts even before we got to him."

"Because you pointed out he was stealing from me, and...other things."

"Yeah, you don't have to remind me. Other than that, the rest of the family shut him out at your word. He got on Bianco's bad side when he tried to do the exchange on his own, after realizing Bianco wanted him to take the fall."

The exchange. When Jimmy went rogue, he inadvertently bought me some time when Tony and Frank were ready to kill me. The irony.

"You didn't bring me here to give me a summary of what I already know."

"Who'd still side with him?"

Kendall shrugs. "I can imagine a couple of my uncles being sympathetic, but everyone has been quiet. Luca and Claudia cooperated too."

"Okay. Tom Foster, Luca? Any connection there?"

"You mean like a relationship? Again, not my organized crime expertise. Tom Foster was out and in a committed relationship. Luca cheated on his wife. Completely different premise."

"I can see that. You knew the partner?"

"I was somewhat aware, that's all. But if you're thinking he's the mysterious player—I think Jimmy and Frank are yanking your chain. Frank could have just given the order to Peck, and that's it."

"But for what?" I am frustrated, and I can't deny it. For a while, my focus was on the murder of Alphonso Mancini, and trying to get Kendall to work with us. It was supposed to be, what, over? I'm not that naïve. We have to be careful, figure out who's trying to snatch a piece of the pie.

"To piss me off? Frank would do that. Jimmy would do it if he could. Occam's Razor, Robyn. You don't have to look that far."

"What you said earlier about sex and mistakes..."

She smiles. It's almost enough to distract me.

"Stay with me here," I say, meaning both of us. "That affair with Claudia was pretty risky. A guy like him, I'd assume there were more women."

"That's really not something I like to think about, but yes, there was talk. He was cheating on Sofia before they even got married."

"And Luca?"

She looks confused. I have to admit I'm fishing at the moment. "What does he have to do with this? Other than cheating on his wife, that is, but he's not a violent guy. I know, he gets talked into bad stuff, but he's not like Frank or Jimmy. Where are you going with this?"

"I wish I knew," I say with a sigh. "I think you are both right and wrong. We have to look in the vicinity of these guys. It's certainly related, but there could be someone else. What is the rule for handling someone having affairs like that? How is access to business regulated?"

I might be fishing, but when I see her pensive look, I think I might be on to something. Yes, I've studied the Mancinis. Not long ago, Peck called me a specific name, *goomar*, a term originally derived from the Italian term for "godmother," but in this form used for a mistress. Kendall and her family, however, are and have always been a special case.

"Okay. You know I didn't use to bring anyone home to meet the family. Most of those women didn't even know who I was."

All of a sudden, it's almost uncomfortably hot in the room. Not that I want to think about her with another woman. Kendall is my wife. She gave up that life to be with me. It's a heady power trip, nothing I ever expected coming out of my assignment.

"All right, so you think Frank might have handled things the same? No offense to you, I'm obviously not comparing the two of you."

"You better not. Everything that happened in my case was completely consensual." She lets the possibilities hang in the air for a few seconds, and I can't help being amused. Kendall is so good at this, and she knows it.

"I don't assume he told them a lot. Sofia knew things because she was used to being quiet and making herself invisible. It would depend on the women's motives. Or, I guess, those of Luca's boyfriend. Boyfriends."

"Could one of them have been trying to take over the family business from the outside?"

"It would be very risky for that person, but not completely unheard of. Sort of like what you did."

"I wasn't going to—" I stop my sentence when I realize she's teasing. "In your opinion, would it be useful to start looking at them?"

"You tell me. I understand you weren't looking into taking over my business, but technically you might have been able to. Remember that the regular mistress or boyfriend probably wouldn't run an operation as sophisticated as the FBI's—but they could try to do some damage."

"Kicking it off with a random execution."

"Two mistakes," Kendall says. "It wasn't random, and it must have started before. Maybe even around the time of Foster's, or my dad's murder. I still say we go back to Frank, and I'll lean harder on Claudia."

I think of something Hampton said a while ago, and I can't say I disagree. It *is* a soap opera with these families—entitlement, wealth, sex. Happily Ever After? We still have a lot of work to do.

"Thank you. You've been a great help. I have some research to do now—see you tonight?"

"Oh, you will. I'm dismissed?" She doesn't wait for an answer, but instead kisses me long enough to make her point.

"Not quite. Wait up for me tonight."

Chapter Ten

O nce in my office, I call *Catania* and ask them to get my table ready for this evening. The next call is to my housekeeper to prepare my outfit for tonight, and then I settle in for some long overdue paperwork.

The conversation we had gave me a lot to think about. For years, I'd been so immersed in grief and obligation—I paid a lot less attention than Robyn and her boss think. Even so, I remember conversations spoken in hushed tones, bits and pieces. My parents discussing Claudia's affair. They weren't going to meddle, but they were incredulous about it.

Jimmy and Dad talking about Tom Foster, Jimmy sneering about something and Dad scolding him. What I told Robyn is true—go for the obvious. People, places, situations. Finally, Arturo Rossi wasn't responsible for the explosion at one of our construction sites a few years ago. It happened around the same time Foster was murdered.

Go for the obvious.

Peck. Adria. The Biancos.

Before I can follow that thought all the way to the end, my phone rings. It's Sandra, my CFO. I was lucky I could shield most of my employees from the prodding of the FBI—they wanted what I could give them. Fortunately,

I had enough to give. I didn't go to prison, and I'm still running the company.

"Kendall, hi. I thought you'd want to have a look at last quarters' numbers."

"Of course. I'll be here all afternoon. You want to come by now?"

"Sure. I'll see you in a bit."

I'm still pondering the significance of those curious connections when she knocks on my door.

"Come on in. Would you like a coffee?"

"No thanks. I'm already dangerously close to walking on the ceiling."

"That bad?"

"Actually no," she says, laying out the contents of the folder she brought, for me. "You were right to let go of Adria. That helped quite a bit."

"I can still keep my condo and go out to dinner every once in a while, then."

I'm sure she was about to roll her eyes at me, but she has enough respect to withhold the urge. I flip through the pages. It's not a complete surprise, but they're still pleasant.

"Looking good," I say. I don't need to add that we're lucky.

Sandra takes a seat.

"Not everyone was happy with the way things went."

"Really? Tell me more."

"I've heard some of the shareholders grumble, and business partners too, but they'll go with what works. The Biancos are over. Arturo has one foot in prison most of the time, and none of the smaller players would have the capacity to go all the way. Hence..." She points a perfectly manicured fingernail at the bottom line which looks quite nice for all of us.

"You've done a great job. Thank you."

"Will this be over at some point?" she asks. "The FBI is still watching us?"

"We are not the focus right now. We still have to be careful, but the worst is behind us."

From that angle, anyway. Peck and whoever paid him is another story.

"Just to be on the safe side, could you make me a list of people who were unhappy? Those who are still doing business with us, and those who stopped. I want to know what exactly I'm dealing with."

"I'll get on it right away. A few were verbal about it, but it's not a long list."

"Even better. Thanks."

Being prepared is more important than ever. I sure as hell don't miss Jimmy, but I do miss the times when he was on top of issues like that, though in retrospect he probably always kept important things from me. I need to replace him, but this will be difficult. Sofia isn't interested in the job, and besides I already gave her one.

Robyn—I laugh at the thought. She would have no reservations rolling her eyes at me, and then some. On a more sober note, I plan to involve her more. Soon. I'm aware I'll have to proceed with caution. Her career could be in jeopardy, even if nothing illegal ever happened.

Sandra sends me the list ten minutes after she left my office. I study it, not surprised at what I see.

When the FBI took me into custody, Luca didn't waste any time meeting with the shareholders. Ever since my mother took over the business, and I did after her, there has been talk. Some of those old-fashioned guys want a "man of the house." I look at the list again, jotting down notes. I might have to give them a talk of my own, get a feel if there's anyone bigoted enough to switch loyalties to the Biancos.

I need to talk to Claudia again.

It doesn't matter if that infamous *Capo dei capi* exists or not. I have to keep my house in order and know without a doubt who helps or hinders.

I call my secretary and ask her to send out a set of invitations. I'm helping the FBI best I can, but I still have a day job.

Chapter Eleven

To my surprise, the detective investigating the shooting, Ashley Carter, comes to see me at the office.

"Agent Johnson, hello. I'm sorry I didn't call first, but I was in the neighborhood. Do you have a moment?"

"Is there any new development on your case?"

Her expression doesn't give anything away. "Perhaps we could talk somewhere in private?"

"My partner, Hampton McKay. He's working with me on our side," I introduce him. "I suppose he should hear it too."

"Sure." Carter shrugs and follows us to the conference room. We close the door behind us, but no one sits. I'm eager to hear the news. With a little luck, this murder isn't related to an onslaught of malice coming our way. An isolated incident.

"I don't know if you're aware that we're also investigating the death of Brad Dolan."

This was not what I expected to hear. "I assumed."

"You had a difficult history with him."

All of a sudden, I wish I hadn't invited Hampton to this conversation. "You read the case files. He nearly killed me, a colleague and a dozen innocent bystanders. I'd call that difficult, but I can save you some time. I didn't kill him."

"We weren't thinking that."

I'm not reassured. "All this happened around the time Judge Lawrence recused herself from Ms. Mancini's case. Judge Collins took over, and suddenly Dolan walked. Someone didn't want him to talk."

"That's what we're thinking. There wasn't much at the crime scene, but I did some research, and found something interesting. There was a suspect in the murder of Tom Foster. He was killed with a gun of the same caliber, not far from the Dolan crime scene, two shots."

"So, you think the third player might exist after all?"

"I'm looking at everyone who had an interest in Dolan's death, and who was friendly with Foster and his partner. Unfortunately, this does point back to Ms. Mancini and her family."

That's what I was afraid of. I have a hard time hiding my impatience.

"Then why are you talking to me instead of Kendall?"

"Oh, we will talk to her, don't worry. I just thought you might have some ideas for me, given your history with Dolan."

"I don't know that I have." I'm aware of Hampton's curious gaze. Kendall and I have enough on our plates, privately and professionally, to give much thought to a dead criminal who had rather sadistic tendencies in life. Now the bastard is going to haunt me from his grave.

"Okay. I'll talk to Elaine Driver as well."

This is just getting worse.

"Why? She left the FBI after the hostage situation. If you want to find out more about Dolan, talk to Judge Collins who, by the way, was found guilty of corruption and conspiracy. There's your connection."

"Just loose ends," she says. "I want her perspective."

I'm not sure what kind of perspective Elaine will be able to give her. We didn't talk all that much after the incident, too scared to rip open wounds, to address vulnerability, mortality.

My feelings for her seemed rather insignificant in that context.

"If you think that helps. I'm sorry, what you read in the reports is all that I can tell you about Dolan. He wanted power, money, and liked to hurt people. That was all there was to him."

"Thank you for your time, Agent Johnson. Agent McKay, nice to meet you. I'll find my way out."

When she's left the room, I consider sitting down, but I need a strong coffee more than anything. Hampton follows me to the break room, waiting. I have nothing to say to him, not now.

"Really? You think this will just blow over?"

Without facing him, I can sense his impatience.

"We have a job to do, so does Carter."

"That's all? Come on, Robyn, she's behind this. You know it." When I don't answer, he adds, "Did you marry her so you could cover it up?"

I spin around, nearly splashing both of us with coffee in the process.

"What the hell is wrong with you?"

"Why would this be so far-fetched? You went to great lengths to keep her out of prison. She owes you, and in her circles, that means something."

"I'm not sure if you're insulting me or her, but I can assure you I never wanted Dolan dead, not that I spent a minute mourning him. I wanted his ass in prison. Were you even paying attention? You know Collins tried to cover his tracks which didn't work."

"The story doesn't end there though. There's still Foster, and the man Peck killed, all pointing back to—"

"The Biancos," I remind him.

"The Mancinis. Robyn, you know this can't work in the long run. Perhaps it's time you take a good hard look at your goals."

"I'll do it when SAC Carr tells me to do so. She brought Kendall on board after our investigation was over. Honestly, you're the one who should take a good hard look at what you're doing. Accusing me of getting a perp executed? That's low."

I pick up my coffee and leave, not waiting for him this time.

—ele—

I do, however, spend the afternoon browsing old files regarding Al Mancini, Tom Foster and what we know about their work together. How they handled the competition. When I meet Kendall at *Catania*, I'm none the wiser, tired, frustrated, and ready for some scrumptious food.

She's sitting at the usual table, studying some files, a glass of red already in front of her. When she sees me, she gets up to greet me with a kiss far too sensual given the fact that we're in public.

It's not melting all of the doubts away. She's told me she had nothing to do with it, but as much as she cares about me, Kendall has lied to me before when she felt like it was necessary to protect me. I've done the same. That's one dilemma we might never be able to solve.

We could have fled the country.

"You look tired," she observes. "Did anything happen?"

"That getaway place, is it still safe?" Her father left her a number in case disappearing would become a last resort. The people offering this service once provided us with a splendid getaway. Come to think of it, it would just be cut short like the last time.

"Of course. I'm sorry you didn't get to have a real honeymoon. I can call tonight if you—"

"No," I interrupt her. "We have too much work here."

"Okay." She closes her files and put them back into a briefcase. "Let's start with dinner then."

"Did Detective Carter reach out to you today?"

"She did," Kendall says calmly. "We had a talk."

"Did you have Dolan killed?"

She sips her wine, unhurried. "You know that if I had, I couldn't tell you. She's looking in all the wrong places, and I told her so. All the work you've done, that we have done together to prevent an all-out war...It's going to be for nothing if they neglect the Biancos and allow them to come back."

Could they? It seems like a fairly obvious attempt at distraction. I think of Hampton's accusation. He hasn't talked much to me since I walked out on him.

"That's bullshit and you know it," I return. "I've seen you at work. I've studied you and your family. You play within the margins most of the time, but your parents made exceptions. So did you."

"So what?"

"Kendall."

She doesn't answer right away as the waiter comes by to refill her glass and bring one for me. He walks away. The silence drags on, confirming what I was afraid to hear. Who was I to think that I could change the system, change her? And am I really innocent in this?

"You didn't ask me to do anything. That's not what I heard when you shared your story. I know you'd never do that. As far as my responsibilities go, I've been fulfilling them. I'm running a legitimate business."

I shake my head. Earlier, she admitted it: She wouldn't tell me the truth.

On the table, Kendall takes my hand.

"This all went very fast. I know you have questions that go far beyond mine or my parents' business practices, but could you be patient with me? Just a little bit longer."

"How long?"

"I don't know."

I have the impulse to get up and walk out on her, but she's still holding my hand.

"I swear to you, this is not going to be a problem for us," she continues. "We have other things to deal with. Peck is still not talking, I assume. The weakest link here is still Luca. Put some pressure on him. We need to contain whatever he or Bianco thinks is going to come our way. There will still be time for everything else."

"Not if Carter busts you."

"She won't."

"What about Foster? Your dad seemed to like him. You think he'd put out a hit on his murderer?"

Kendall gives a heartfelt sigh. "You know what, he might have. I have no idea. Could we enjoy dinner now?"

Food and sex will always be the perfect escape. I postpone the questions for the time being, but I won't be able to put them off forever. Kendall is in a mood tonight, a lot more optimistic than I am about the future.

I let her take over. I like it way too much.

Chapter Twelve

I'm still on a high from the possibilities. The present is extremely promising as well, Robyn's skin hot under my fingertips as I trace them down her back. We both needed the intense intimacy, the glorious exhaustion that comes with it. I needed her like this to make my point clear.

But I'm not in the mood to talk yet, so I lean in and kiss her, and she turns to pull me on top of her.

"See how life doesn't have to be complicated?"

Robyn laughs, her expression more joyous than I've seen it in some time. I'm feeling the joy.

"I can never tell what you're up to." She's not really complaining at this moment.

"Keeping you happy, for starters. Keeping the peace."

"What does that mean?"

I asked for it. Instead of going for another round of passionate lovemaking, I pull her into an embrace. Now might be a good time to address this, make sure she's ready.

Frank and Jimmy think a storm is coming, they might be right. They just don't know the direction it's coming from.

"I did comply with everything, got rid of Adria, cleaned up the Mancini Group."

"I know. I was there," she mumbles against my chest.

"Right. I'm not kidding myself into thinking that Carr gave me the consulting job for any other reason than keeping tabs on me. Let her, I'm okay with that. But I need to do things my way to a certain extent. It's the only way it will work."

"I'm not sure I understand what you're saying. You might have blown my mind earlier."

"Much as I enjoy the praise, it's not so complicated. I have to talk to a few people. Not everyone came back to do business with us after we got rid of the Biancos. It's time for some consequences." I can't help being amused at the alarm in her eyes. "As in, making sure we reward the ones who stuck by us and limit business with the ones who didn't. What were you thinking? No, don't answer that. I just want to make sure that people know there's no vacuum, no room for small petty men to take control."

"Sounds good and also foolishly dangerous to some extent," she muses. "You're going to keep it legal."

"I hope that wasn't a question, and I'm offended by the foolishly dangerous."

"Sorry about that. Will you accept my sincere apologies?"

My heart is beating faster as I'm learning said apology won't be a verbal one, her hands traveling over my body with intent.

So be it.

"Let's see what you've got," I say before her mouth is on mine, initiating a kiss that's deep and messy and magnificent—just like everything else between us.

⁓ℓℓ⁓

I'm done with the Bureau for the week unless they call me in. I know Robyn will be busy looking into Frank's extramarital affairs, among other things. I feel only a pang of guilt for not giving her too many details about the meeting I've called at *Catania*. I'll tell her all about it eventually, but I want to see how it goes first. She's having dinner with Hampton and his family.

Claudia is the first to arrive.

"Good evening, Mrs. Johnson," she greets me. "Your wife isn't here?"

I roll my eyes at her. "Not tonight. Frankly, that's a lot of attitude for someone who made plans with our good friend Arturo behind my back."

So I got her brother arrested. I think we're more than even given that she's still on the payroll, and still doing restaurant business on her own now that we sold the Adria Group.

"I know I'm never going to live that down, but I was too curious," she admits.

"Good. You won't regret it."

Sofia is next to arrive. They shake hands with an air of caution. I direct them to the family table and go to check on the orders for the evening. I know everything will be perfect. It's more like another excuse to check the parking, and this time I'm rewarded. The woman getting out of her car holds her head up high, approaching the door with a determined stride. Luca's wife is the least likely to forgive me, but at least she came. We've communicated through secretaries, so I'm not sure yet how this will go. When she enters the restaurant, I go to greet her.

"Good evening, Elena. I'm so glad you could make it."

"I was wondering what we'd have to talk about and couldn't come up with anything. I admit you got me intrigued."

"It's not much of a secret, but you'll see. The others are here, so why don't we start with dinner?"

She shrugs but doesn't disagree.

So far so good.

Elena sits down at the table with the others, but I stand. There's significance in that. Even with wine and appetizers on the table. They're cold, though. I'll be done once it's time for the main course.

I look at the women looking back at me with expressions ranging from curiosity to suspicion—they're right not to underestimate me. I don't tolerate ridicule, but they're still family, and in the aftermath of recent mayhem, they've done their best to help keep the family business together.

Well, even Claudia did after some prompting. I don't hand out that many second chances, but I'm willing to give her this one. Sofia has been steadfast. Elena certainly felt like she had to keep up appearances, but she, too has had a hard time which has more to do with Luca's actions before he went to prison.

"Thank you all for coming. I have something important to share, and I wanted you to be the first ones to know."

"You're pregnant!" Claudia exclaims, and I nearly roll my eyes at her again.

"Let's be serious for a moment. This *is* serious. You all know about the shooting at the restaurant, and a possible connection to the murder of Tom Foster." I get no objection from them.

"It has to stop there. It will. But for that, whoever's vying for power needs to understand that there is no room. We are all still here, and if we continue to work together, we can contain them."

"How, if we don't know who they are?" Sofia asks, Claudia speaking at the same time, "I thought you didn't want to do things the usual way anymore."

Elena looks pensive.

I hold up a hand. "First of all, we'll find out. The FBI is on the case. They don't want interference either, and they have the means to get to the bottom of this."

"Meaning, your wife."

"It doesn't matter. We'll figure it out, but meanwhile, we must present a united front. I have a list here, and you might have heard things—these are people who have become very chummy with folks close to the Biancos. For future transactions, I want you to avoid them."

Elena's eyes widen when she reads the list. She exchanges a look with Claudia.

"Some of those names have been supplying the business for decades."

"Yes, and they won't be anymore. We need to draw the line somewhere." I know that at least two of my guests are itching for a confrontation, so I'm pre-empting it. "I know I've made mistakes. We all have, at some point." Claudia drinks deeply from her glass. "But working with the FBI to get the Biancos out of the way wasn't. Too much violence, too many drugs, too many deaths. This is not what my father wanted, or Lorenzo, and it's not how we ever did business." It wasn't always completely void of violence, or death, but it was limited, targeted. There's a difference. "I thought it was important to start with you. Let's show them that it doesn't take a man necessarily to get things done."

I halt, take a moment to gauge how effective my pitch was. They are all smart capable women. I know that the statement hits home with them in various ways.

"Well, some of us have to do without since you got my husband thrown in jail."

I can tell Claudia barely keeps herself from snickering at Elena's comment.

"True, there is that. If Luca hadn't teamed up with Jimmy, and run a drug ring out of Adria, he'd still be available. We need to get past this. I know he was worried about appearances and Uncle Lorenzo's approval, but that's not enough to justify what he did. We've all been stalled in various ways. Some people still think

I should have married Jimmy after everything he did. Claudia—we all know what happened with Frank."

"What happened with Frank?" she asks coolly. She's not entirely convincing. Sofia is listening carefully.

"The other day when we talked, you were afraid. We can help you if we all stick together."

"That is not a small thing to ask," Elena says.

"I'm aware. But it's either that or we leave it all to chance, and someone close to the Biancos, or, eventually one of them, will wreak havoc in the city. We barely avoided it the last time. We can make this permanent. Claudia, you will be protected like Sofia is. And Elena, you don't have to spend another day in Luca's shadow."

"I'm so angry at you, Kendall."

I figured. We have exchanged few words since Luca's arrest, and her emotions must be all over the place. She had some kind of peace before, but it was fragile.

"I know. And I'm sorry for the hurt I caused you, but I'm not sorry for stopping him. You all know that Dad wouldn't have tolerated this."

"Maybe not, but you were lucky. Luca wasn't. His father would have never accepted him the way yours did."

"I'm aware. However, what he did, to the business, and to you, had nothing to do with being gay. He made a lot of money on the side, for no one but himself."

Elena sighs. "I hate that you are right. I certainly didn't see any of that money, not that I would have wanted it. I always thought we had more than enough with what we made off the real estate and the actual restaurant business. You really think Frank Bianco is still a threat?"

Both Sofia and Claudia flinch, for different reasons or the same, I'm not sure.

"That's what we're going to find out. If it's him or someone else, we need to be ready. All of us. I'd like us to coordinate with future big decisions regarding the company. Let's share if we hear anything that's out of the ordinary. Eventually, I'd like to have Marc and Anna in this too, and we'll go back to doing family dinners. Just not with the separation of coffee and dessert for women, smokes and drinks for men."

Claudia laughs. "Right, like we couldn't always use a drink on those nights."

"I think it would help create some stability," Sofia offers. "Let them know someone's in charge. I'm in."

Perhaps she means to challenge Claudia, too, because her story with Frank Bianco is crystal clear while Claudia's still isn't.

"Sure, me too," Claudia says with a shrug. "We have all cleaned up after my brother got himself caught. We'll have the FBI on our side, and we aren't paying bribes." It's my turn to flinch. "Sounds like a good deal."

"Elena?"

She hesitates for a few seconds before she nods. "I guess it can't harm. I'll get you everything you need."

Finally, I sit down. "I promise you, that's only the beginning. Now, let's celebrate."

This is what I've wanted to do for a long time. And someday not far from now, Robyn will be at the table with us. It might be complicated to get there, but we will.

No one's skipping town.

I'm not done.

Chapter Thirteen

Hampton's invitation came as a bit of a surprise, given that our recent interactions have been quite frosty. I'm even more surprised to realize his wife isn't home.

"You're okay with ordering in?" he asks as we sit down in the living room.

"Sure. I'm curious. Is this an intervention of one?" I try to keep my tone light, non-accusatory. We still have to work together, and we're still friends—I hope.

"No, just a couple of friends hanging out after work. Would you like a beer?"

"Yes, please."

"Be right back."

He brings a couple of bottles—my favourite, I realize—and a take-out menu from the kitchen. We both choose, and he makes the call. When that is done, an awkward silence settles between us, until we both speak at the same time.

"I'm sorry," he starts.

"I don't want this to be a recurring subject," I say at the same time. "We'll keep work and home life separate best we can, but it was Rachel who invited Kendall. So far, it's working. We get to know what she knows."

"It sounds good in theory," he admits.

"You're not convinced. I'm not supposed to keep an eye on her anymore. She's my wife. She'll be in when and if we need her, nothing more. Things have changed."

"You have taught me a lot in the time we've worked together."

"Thank you?" If it sounds more like a question, it's because I know that won't be all, and I'm not sure where he's going with this.

"I mean it. I always thought you were one of the sharpest most level-headed people in the field. That's why I can't understand."

"I just tried to explain."

"And the fact that a man was shot in front of you, days after your wedding, doesn't bother you?"

"What kind of question is that? Kendall didn't shoot him, nor did she order anyone to do it." I'm uncomfortably reminded of Detective Carter's questions regarding Dolan and Kendall's reluctance to give me a straight answer. Regardless, I know for certain that she's not connected to Peck or whoever sent him.

"She's in over her head, Robyn, and she'll always be. Comes with the territory. Perhaps the Mancinis can run a business that looks clean on paper, but they will always be connected. The circumstances surrounding Dolan's death are still odd."

"Oh, come on. I thought we were past that."

"What if this whole thing about a third player is just a distraction?"

"That's the theory as far as I'm concerned. Kendall doesn't believe in him either. Just some smokescreens from the Biancos."

"What if it's not the Biancos behind those smoke-screens?"

The doorbell rings, and he gets up to get the food, leaving me to ponder what exactly he means by that. He doesn't trust Kendall. She has doubts about him. Pity, they'll just have to live with the fact that because of me, they'll be in each other's lives in some way. Kendall has her hands full. She spent the last few years grieving both of her parents and battling homophobia and sexism thrown at her from both "friends" and foes.

Al Mancini didn't want her to rule the city, he wanted to come clean and lay the groundwork for his daughter to run a respectable business.

Hampton brings the food and another couple of beers. At least something's going to soften the blow.

"You think it's Kendall who wants a comeback? You're underestimating her. She's aware that she's still under a lot of scrutiny and perhaps always will be. Besides, it's Jimmy and Luca who have been spreading rumors about that bigshot player and worrisome things to come."

Hampton sighs. "I know you won't believe this but keep it in mind as a working theory. She gave us Luca Mancini, yes, but only when she needed an out and could no longer deny what he did. She let Bruno get away the first time."

"In order to take care of me. This is getting a bit too much, even counting the free meal."

"If you find out I'm right..."

"What do you think I'll do? You're wrong. There's nothing shady going on. We're just trying to find some peace after everything."

He nods, though I'm certain he's not convinced.

"I hope you'll find it. To peace,"

We clink our bottles together. I can't be sure about Dolan, but if that's the only doubt left, I'll learn to live with it. I have a job to do. That doesn't mean I can't be happy with the woman I love.

Chapter Fourteen

Claudia lingers after Sofia and Elena have left, gazing out of the window absent-mindedly. I return to the table and sit across from her.

"Did you ever feel like you've done something so stupid that you could never recover from it no matter what you do?"

For a short time, yes, but then I realized I couldn't imagine my life without Robyn in it—and she kept her side of the bargain, helped me find my father's killer. But that's not the same.

"I have," I acknowledge anyway. "I let myself get carried away as I'm sure you have, not that she tried to hurt me."

"Not physically anyway."

"She was doing her job at first, and that didn't turn out too badly for all of us. Frank doesn't have that excuse."

"What you said makes sense. I don't know if I can ever sit across from Sofia and not be ashamed."

It's a valid emotion. Sofia's story was hardly a secret.

"Looking back, I can hardly believe myself," she continues. "I had a tough time. I couldn't see beyond that."

"The important thing is how we move forward. Sofia, Elena, you, and me. I don't want any more misunderstandings."

"We haven't given you enough credit," she says. "Luca and Dad had this toxic kind of relationship, and I always thought I was outside of it. Considering the whole story, Frank, and doing business with Arturo, it's pretty clear that I was wrong."

"We can either cower or show them who's in charge. I prefer the latter. What?" I ask when she studies me, her gaze pensive.

"I can't help being a bit jealous," she admits. "I'm grateful I managed to clean up my marriage but...Wow. She is good for you."

That statement brings a bit of warmth to my face, for multiple reasons.

"Yes, she is."

—ele—

When we part ways in front of *Catania*, there's no message from Robyn yet, so she's still with McKay. I take the time to go back to the Mancini Group's headquarters where I sit in my office, alone, with a glass of whiskey I keep for special occasions, the city in lights below me.

For the first time in a long time, I feel like I can take a deep breath. Everything is going to be all right. I've been mad at all of them except for Sofia. I had my reasons. They are coming home, and so will the rest of the family.

The legacy will continue.

Maybe, one day, there will be grandchildren running around at *Catania*. Much of it depends on the next steps. Robyn.

If it was only for SAC Carr, I might have politely declined the offer and lived with the consequences, but given where we were at that point, it was no longer an option.

I can't wait until I can introduce her to the future, but I'll have to be patient a little while longer. I raise my glass, toasting to myself. Right. I must get a bunch of old-fashioned guys and their sons on board—piece of cake.

They won't have much of a choice if their pride in the Mancini family name is greater than the one in some of those antiquated attitudes.

I come home to find Robyn already in PJs, watching the news.

"Hey," I say, leaning down to kiss her. "How was your evening, Agent Johnson?"

"Okay," she answers vaguely. "How was your girls' night out?" I didn't have to say much—she knows all about my complicated history with these women. What she doesn't know is that she has an important part in the endgame.

Marriage was a first great step, but I have to be careful. I can't spook her, or all my efforts will be for nothing.

"I'd be right to assume that along with the girl-talk, there was some scheming going on?"

"I knew I couldn't keep anything from you," I return as I sit next to her. My frustration isn't entirely feigned. She did see right through me.

"It was easy to spot." She laughs. "You only call me Agent Johnson when you're trying to keep something from me."

"I'm not. You've seen the way I work. I'm kind of tired swimming upstream. It's not so easy for someone in my position to find allies, but those come closest. Sofia is beyond reproach. The others are...inclined. Good enough for now."

Robyn ponders my words. I know they make sense to her because she's studied families like mine. She knows that consolidation will send a signal. A house divided is an invitation for trouble.

"This is what your parents were hoping for."

"I believe so. I think Dad realized it was the only way to make peace, even though it came with risks."

"Are you going to find it? Peace?"

"I already have it. It's right here." Frustration aside, it is true. Maybe it is exactly what I have always needed—someone who knows me. And I'm grateful she came to me.

Chapter Fifteen

Frank Bianco doesn't get many visitors. I cross a few names off my list, wondering if this is the right direction. His family is under observation, and those are the few members not in prison.

He used to gamble, drink, had several affairs. He cheated on his wife, and on his mistresses as well. A few years ago, he'd been dating an older woman named Marla Colvin, the daughter of a contractor. There were other women, but she stayed by his side for three years, loyal like most of the actual wives in those families. Like Elena Mancini.

I sit back, once more astonished. I know Sofia's story pretty well by now. It's still remarkable that Al and Angela Mancini didn't blink. They were there for her when she needed help, and they did a lot to extend the work of the foundation that is still a part of the Mancini group. The fact that she got away, that she got help is definitely an outlier in this context.

Without getting ahead of myself, I still think that this is a relevant fact.

I drop by Marla Colvin's house in the early afternoon, unannounced. She hasn't been to court. Laying low, making plans? Or maybe she was as naïve about their relationship as Claudia before. There are still a lot of connections between the Mancinis and the Biancos, undeniable despite their mutual disdain.

She opens the door of the impressive home in a robe, with a Martini in hand.

"I'm Agent Robyn Johnson with the FBI. I have a few questions regarding Frank Bianco."

I almost expected her to slam the door in my face, but to my surprise, she steps aside after giving my badge a curious glance.

"Come on in, sweetie. I never miss an occasion to tell the world how much of an asshole Frank is."

That is...interesting.

"What did he do now?" she asks. "He's still locked up I hope?"

"Yes, don't worry. He's not going to get out anytime soon."

"Good. The world is a better place for it. You care for a drink?"

"I'm on the clock. Sorry."

She gives me a long look that's almost sympathetic. "Didn't stop all of those who came knocking before you. What do you want to know, sweetie?"

"You and Frank dated for about three years, is that right?"

"God, was it that long? I suppose you're right. He cheated on me on our second date."

"I'm sorry," I say though I can't help thinking, what did she expect dating a married man? One whose wife fled from him. "Aside from him being an...asshole, what was the day-to-day life like? Did he ever bring other women to the house? Was it an open secret?"

She shakes her head. "It was no secret at all, and my family never stopped chiding me for getting involved with a man like that. I was offended—I was an adult after all—but I have to say they were right."

"You think any of his mistresses had access to the business, records, accounts etc.?" His other mistresses. I don't say it out loud. I seem to have gained her trust, and she elaborates,

"I'm not sure they did, but they certainly saw the appeal of money. He used to buy me a lot of gifts. That's how I knew he'd slept with someone else. Sometimes he brought them over for dinner, pretending it was for work. They had a gleam in their eyes, but he never agreed to a divorce from Sofia."

"So, he was stringing them along while punishing Sofia at the same time." Marla doesn't question my assessment. "I hear that he was angry. Did he ever take that anger out on you?"

For the first time, her expression darkens. The humor is gone. I'm beginning to understand why she's drinking at this time of day.

"Frank took out his anger when, and on whom he chose to at any time. Which resulted in more gifts and bribes, because, I'm sure you know, that's how his family operates."

It sounds like a lot more people had reasons to hate him rather than try to help and protect him. That might still be a viable lead.

"Of those other women, do you think any one of them would support him now?"

"What do I know?" she asks with a shrug. "Women fall in love with serial killers. It's possible."

"You have names?"

"A few."

I wait as she picks up a pen and notebook, wondering...I'm still inclined to go with Kendall's theory. But what if someone wanted to frame Bianco? If it's Marla, what would be the endgame? I don't know enough about her, but she seems content to live a life away from him.

There are others who have the ambition and the means to take power. Sofia. Claudia.

Kendall.

No. I can't believe it. We asked her to give up Frank, his father, and the rest of the clan, so she did.

Marla tears a page off the notebook and hands it to me. "Of course, those are just the ones during my time...There are certainly more."

"Thank you for talking to me. You have a lovely home," I tell her as she walks me back to the front door.

It's true. Her surroundings scream luxury and taste. It's a bit too much of a non-sequitur, I realize.

"You're asking if Frank bought it for me?" She laughs bitterly. "I believe the state would own it by now. No, I was lucky to meet a better man eventually. Have a good day, Agent Johnson. I hope you'll make sure Frank stays where he is."

We have a common goal here.

When I'm on the way to my car, Kendall texts me.

Will you be home for dinner?

I think of the names to run, dates to check. Tonight is not the night for a quiet evening in—or out.

Sorry, I'll probably be late.

That's okay. The answer comes right away. *I'll find something to occupy myself with.* Winking emoji. This could mean so many things, some of which I might not want to know about. Some that bring the heat to my face. I laugh at myself. All things considered, I'm extremely lucky.

Back at the office I run the names that Marla gave me. I find nothing out of the ordinary. Next, I go online, and

I find a picture of one of them, Lucy Yates, with Judge Collins.

"I'll be damned," I say out loud, prompting a curious look from Hampton. He comes over, and I show him the screen. "Take a look. That's one of Bianco's mistresses from the time he was officially dating Marla Colvin. She's Collins' niece."

"Circumstantial," he says with a shrug.

"Collins had a long-standing relationship with the Biancos. There's got to be something there."

"You're fishing. Find a connection to Peck, then we'll talk."

He's right, I have to give him that. But it's a start. I'm happy about every lead that points away from Kendall, because really, what would I do?

I return to my search rather than trying to answer that question. Most likely, I already did.

Chapter Sixteen

Three things happen in quick succession: First, I get a call from an investigative reporter who offers to ghost-write my autobiography. I politely decline, not for a lack of ego, but because I'm too busy—with the second. We've done a great job streamlining and consolidating the business. It's time for a bold move.

Third, I've decided to involve Robyn sooner than originally planned. There haven't been any other executions, and she's still working on finding the mystery third player who might be trying to restore old Bianco glory.

We have a goal in common, aside from the fact that we promised forever. That matters above all, and I have to admit it's still making me nervous.

At these meetings, nothing illegal has happened *per se*. I check in with family, show them the numbers, proving that I'm perfectly capable of running things without a man by my side, let alone letting him do the job. Tradition has its merits, but we use what works.

I do have a partner, and tonight will be her official introduction.

She doesn't know it yet. I took her to a family dinner early on, and of course some family members came to the wedding. This is different. Everyone, including Robyn, will see the difference clearly.

I thought about calling that number again and taking everyone to the safe place that Dad arranged a long time ago, but it's not the time.

Having *Catania* closed to the public for the evening and having everyone over there will send a message.

When I return from the bathroom and start to get dressed, Robyn is still lounging on the bed, blissfully distracting. She's still naked, her hair tousled.

"You're on a roll," she observes. "Don't get me wrong, I love dining at *Catania*, but is this a special occasion I forgot about?"

"It's a surprise. You heard anything new about the mistress angle?"

"No." She sighs and moves to get up. "Several people have better motives for setting Frank up rather than helping him. If it's them, we don't know much more. Peck isn't talking, Collins is stonewalling, and his niece is nowhere to be found. Apparently, he doesn't know where she is."

"Convenient," I say, running my hand down her back as she passes me by, then pull her to me.

"Oh no. If you want me to be ready at six, this is not happening."

"We could miss cocktails. That wouldn't be so bad, would it?"

Warm skin under my hands and lips is too tempting. I can tell she's tempted. A lot depends on tonight, so I let her go reluctantly.

At this moment, we are determining the direction for the business, and a generation of our family. That's a lot of responsibility. For me. For my wife, the FBI agent.

I wonder if she would ever consider quitting. Or, at least, work for another division, though another supervisor might not have the vision of a SAC Carr.

"What?" she asks, sensing my mixed emotions.

"Nothing. I'll give you time to get ready now."

She leans in to kiss me, testing my resolve once more.

I have an announcement to make to the family. I can't be distracted.

—ele—

"I didn't think tonight was about work?" Robyn asks, surprised at my outfit. She's wearing a lilac-colored dress, her hair wound up. I hope no one misunderstands the image we want to project tonight. She isn't overdressed for a formal evening with the family. I had to choose something more sober.

I can't leave anyone in doubt about who's in charge. The past couple of weeks have been promising. I've talked to various family members outside the circle of determined women.

I can't let up now.

"Can't you see there's some glitter in my top?" I'm half joking. There's a bit of sparkle in the black. Tonight isn't just somber. It's about a new beginning, a new era. "Do you want to have children with me?"

"Whoa. As in plural? Where did that come from?"

I know she's not sure how to take my question.

"Would you?"

"Those children would sure lead interesting lives," Robyn muses. "Yes. Of course."

The rush of joy is rather surprising. Could it be that easy?

"Good. It's in the plan, then."

"What am I missing here?"

"You'll know everything after tonight. I swear."

I can see the brief flash of frustration on her face, barely noticeable. There have been many secrets between us, from the start. Convenient ones, necessary ones. This will end. It has to, before we can start a family of our own.

"Everything, huh?"

"Everything."

Robyn picks up the perfume bottle on the vanity.

"Hampton thinks you might be trying to set up Frank. I told him I'm pretty sure that's not the case after we asked you for dirt on him."

"You're right about that. Why would I want to set him up? If I never hear his name again, it would be fine by me."

If there's any conflicting message in this, she doesn't call me out on it. Hampton's musings are no surprise to me either.

"To send a message to everyone who wants to start something," she suggests.

In a way, it's a relief to hear that. It will all come together in a matter of hours.

"My love, if I want to send a message, it won't have anything to do with Frank. He's done, and so is the rest of the clan. I won't start small—especially when we'll have to think about getting another college fund underway."

"Please tell me I won't go to prison for helping to commit tax fraud, and for helping to cover it up?"

I can't help it, I'm laughing.

"Before you ask, yes, it is funny. That's not going to happen, because I couldn't be any more transparent with my finances after the FBI and the IRS examined every bank statement in the history of this company." Okay, that's an exaggeration. For the past ten years or so. "What's more important is that you kept me out of prison at great cost for you. I won't ever forget that. Trust me a little?"

"I love you," she says which doesn't answer my question, stepping closer. "I trust you."

VENGEANCE

That's all I need.

—ele—

It's a lot like the old days, when I was much younger—though the air was thick with smoke back then, and it's a miracle that those of us who were kids at the time came out of it still healthy.

I've had many conversations since the meeting with Claudia, Elena and Sofia, some difficult, others easier.

I catch a glimpse of Uncle Eduardo and Aunt Nina sitting at one of the tables. He's one of the family members who has stayed under the radar through it all. He told me he wasn't interested in hearing about "my lifestyle," "just get the job done." Which is my intention. With some of them it's as good as it gets. Another cousin, Louisa, came out to me.

Times are changing, and we are ready.

"This is the surprise?" Robyn asks, amused. "You took me to dinner with your family a while ago. They know we're married."

"Of course. That's not what it's about," I say, placing a quick kiss on her lips. "You'll see. It's nothing nefarious—but good news. I wanted you to be here when I announce it."

We take our table which is strategically placed. No coincidences tonight.

When everyone is provided with a glass of champagne, I get to my feet and clink a spoon against my glass.

"Could I have your attention for a moment? I swear it won't be long before you can go back to food and drinks." There's some laughter. Robyn's gaze is pensive.

"It's no secret that we've gone through troubled times. We've had terrible losses. So, Mom and Dad, Uncle Lorenzo, and Marina, this is dedicated to you." I'm feel-

99

ing generous tonight, including Uncle Lorenzo whose prejudice made life a lot harder for Luca, and by proxy, all of us. But this is for the long run. For the family.

"I wanted to thank all of you for supporting me in recent weeks. Business is better than ever which tells me we are doing the right thing. For sure, some of our former business partners don't like the transparency, because it puts a spotlight on their business practices as well. That's frankly...not our problem. The Mancini Group is shaping up to have its best quarter in years. Wait a minute," I instruct when some start clapping. "Not yet. There's more good news. Arturo Rossi has retired from the family business effective immediately and has sold his interests to me. What this means in practice is that we will apply the same measures there as we did here. It means cleaner and more transparent business for everyone."

Now it's so quiet you could hear the proverbial pin drop. I've talked about options with the inner circle, but for most of them this is news. Rossi has for a long time tried to put his finger on the scale, trying to earn favors with Tony Bianco. That's all over. If Frank wanted to try something, or anyone else, they know now that the playing field has changed.

"We'll have several meetings in the coming weeks so the transition for our new employees goes as smoothly as possible. Now, let's honor this family tradition and have the best food in the world outside the real Catania."

A few of them stop by to congratulate me on the acquisition. Everyone in the room knows what it means.

Dad was in negotiations with Rossi once, but then they found out about Sofia. The deal was off.

Today, it's no longer a business deal but a capitulation on Rossi's side.

It's a good day.

"How did you do that?" Robyn asks after things quiet down for a bit. Everyone has returned to their tables.

"What do you mean?"

"I've met Rossi. He was trying to team up with Claudia to hurt you. He handed his business over to you, just like that?"

"See, that's why I wanted you to be here, so you know I'm not keeping anything from you. He's tired. His old connections are gone, or in prison. In the end, he agreed that it was the most sensible solution for everyone. And with Sofia having the role she has at the Mancini Group, I can help them transition."

"I was right. Send a message."

"That, too. There weren't any more shootings, and no third player has emerged, right? I think that whoever needed to receive that message, they understood it."

"It's risky. We still don't know who hired Peck."

"We will eventually, but in the meantime, we have to live." I pick up the bottle and refill her glass.

"Sounds like a good plan," Claudia, who has appeared at our table, says ruefully. "Robyn, can I talk to you?"

Robyn shoots me a quizzical glance.

I shrug and get up. "Let's do this somewhere more private."

There's a back room in *Catania* that has seen many functions. Right now, it's only to escape the celebrations for a moment so the two of them can get on the same page. I hope.

"You're looking into Frank's former mistresses," Claudia begins. "I can tell you where to look. Marla Colvin."

"I've talked to her. She's married, lives in a huge house with her husband—and I don't think there's any love lost between her and Frank. We do have another lead though," Robyn answers, her tone carefully neutral.

"Forget about that lead. I've asked around...and I'm pretty sure that she has a lot more answers for you."

"Why do you think that? A hunch?"

"You could say that. Some thought Marla's brother might have been involved in the murder of Tom Foster. He disappeared...then turned up dead."

"Why am I hearing about this for the first time? This wasn't in Foster's case file, and none of the detectives seemed to know about it."

Robyn sounds irritated now, and I don't blame her. The grapevine among families like ours runs deep. It's entirely possible that the investigators never found the connection.

"He had a different father, and they weren't seen together often. Anyway, there's your connection to Foster. I don't know if she or the brother knew Peck, but you should look into that."

"We will, don't worry."

I can tell that Robyn is still wondering about how Marla could have gotten caught up in yet another murder case, after escaping from Frank Bianco's influence. Claudia must have gotten the same sense.

"You'll find that money, power, or both, is always the answer."

Robyn looks troubled for a moment, before she says, "Thank you, Claudia. This is helpful."

"You're welcome. I won't say that Kendall hasn't twisted my arm, but I know I have a lot to make up for. Frank is vicious, and Marla never had a problem with that. Somebody should keep an eye on them. Oh, and congratulations, Kendall."

"Thank you," I say. "I think it's time we all get more champagne."

Conversations in the backroom of Catania, Claudia sharing information with her, Robyn understands that there has been a shift. We have something to celebrate.

It's all for her. Now, she's in.

Chapter Seventeen

I can't deny it—it's a bit of a rush when I read the room and realize what Kendall just did. I thought our wedding would be the biggest change. It might have been, for us personally, but then there's Kendall Mancini's public persona. I've been officially introduced to the family.

I sense it from the way they look at me, with a different kind of respect in their expression and tone when they talk to me.

The time for doubt is over—after the FBI investigation, after paying millions to the IRS, Kendall has taken control. From the looks of it, there's been no real opposition.

Lorenzo, her father's brother, was killed by the Bianco family.

His son, Luca, is in prison, and so is Alphonso's former right-hand man.

Cousin Claudia has a lot to make up for since she plotted, albeit for a short time, against Kendall.

Sofia has had her promotion, but she wouldn't dream of plotting against Kendall.

Here we are.

"Please, don't make this complicated," Kendall says with a bright smile as she hands me another glass of champagne. "This is how we do things. In the end, we come together for the greater good."

"The greater good meaning that you come out on top again."

"We." She corrects me before giving me a speculative gaze that makes my face heat. "Unless you meant something else. We'll get to that later."

"You're trying to change the subject."

"And you're too easy," she says, reaching out to touch my cheek, her fingers cool against my skin. "This is business. In order to keep the company together and enable the foundation to do the good that it does, there needs to be clarity. Look around. This is clarity."

"Everyone knows their place."

"True. And your place is right beside me. That's what we chose, right?"

There's a small trace of...something, doubt, a vulnerability that Kendall rarely shows. A moment ago, I was ready to tear her clothes off, now my heart goes out to her. It's nothing new. My feelings for her will always be a feverish irresistible mix of emotions.

"Yes, we did. This...It's a bit of a surprise, but I guess I should have expected it."

"You're part of the family."

Kendall holds my gaze. We both understand that there are several possible interpretations to this.

"Will I have to quit my job and be a kept woman?" It's not entirely the joke I meant it to be. Or did I?

"You'll be safe whatever you choose to do." That's a bit cryptic and not as decisive a denial as I would have hoped.

"Nothing illegal is going on, and no one will ask you to do anything illegal," she adds. "I guess you could say you'll represent the House of Mancini that fortunately hasn't fallen, and we'll make sure it never does."

I can't help it, I have to laugh. "I've had too much champagne for this to make sense, but I think it's good—right?"

Kendall pulls me close for a kiss. "So good," she whispers. It occurs to me how much more at ease she is around her extended family than she used to be. I'm happy for her, for us. There's been another, no less important shift. Her cousin Lousia whom I hadn't met until now, brought her girlfriend to the gathering. I direct my attention back to the matter at hand.

"Another question. Would you mind if I wanted to quit my job at some point?" Too much champagne, definitely. I haven't forgotten the conversation with Claudia though. We might have to lean harder on Marla Colvin. That is something I will have to bring from the family gathering to the job.

"What would you like to do instead?"

That's a good question. Kendall knows as well as I do what it's like when the path in life was always outlined from the start. Her, inheriting the Mancini empire. Me, inheriting...what exactly? To try and be on the right side of the law? I still am, aren't I?

To put love and loyalty above all else?

"I don't know. You found a job for Jessica Byrne."

"Well, that was an unpaid internship, and she wasn't even real," she sums up my undercover persona. I can't blame her for that.

"It's not something I need to decide right now. I might become a PI."

"I'll let you know when I need an in-house investigator."

That wasn't quite how I meant it, but it might work too. Once upon a time, I considered Hampton a friend, but he and Ryan Farmer have been openly skeptical of my recent choices. Sometime soon, it might be time to move on, even if Kendall keeps her dubious role as a consultant for the Organized Crime unit.

"I might be available."

"Good to know. Now I really need to eat something before we can celebrate some more."

I follow her to the table, more excited than I thought about those options. I no longer have any doubts. Whatever the future holds, it will be with her.

Chapter Eighteen

R obyn took the news better than I thought. Maybe that's because this time, I truly didn't keep anything from her. This is how we work. Run things. Represent. Don't let anyone believe for a second that we can't do it—especially not old-fashioned macho men who are head of family or want to be.

I'm back in my office the next day, at my usual time. I had to leave my tempting—and naked—wife in bed, and no one will bring me coffee and a pastry unless I order first. Other than that, life is splendid. Perfect. With no incident following the shooting, we can almost imagine it had nothing to do with us at all.

Robyn and her team will figure it out with the local cops, and none of that will impede the operations at the Mancini Group. Word is out on the street and in the boardrooms. We are on top, as Robyn worded it, and we intend to stay there.

I send a breakfast order to the kitchen, smiling to myself as I remember *her* on top, late last night.

I always tried to do the most logical thing, the one that made the most sense. Marrying her is at the top of that list. It's been good for business, for rekindling bruised relationships within my own family, but most of all, she is good for my soul.

The phone rings, and I'm still smiling when I pick up. It's Sandra calling, and lately she has had nothing but good news for me. At six in the morning, with coffee and a warm cinnamon muffin on the way, there's hardly a better start to the day, is there?

The smile slips from my face when I hear the voice, and my heart starts hammering.

Not Sandra.

None of the usual suspects. I don't recognize the speaker, but his words send a chill down my spine.

"There's no place for you. Step down—or she dies."

"Who is this?"

"You don't need to know," he scoffs. "I will call you with instructions. Be careful about your next move, and no police."

I wasn't born yesterday. I'm pissed off and scared for Sandra. People like him rarely hesitate. But they also underestimate people like me.

On a secure line I call Sofia, Claudia and Elena in for a meeting. I let only a few seconds of doubt tick by before my next call goes to Robyn. I need her here, in any capacity possible. She's part of the inner circle now, and it's about time I treat her that way.

Robyn picks up after three rings, unaware of the emergency.

"Hey. You miss me already?"

I do, but I can't focus on that now.

"Okay, listen to me carefully. We don't have much time."

"Is everything okay?" she asked, instantly alarmed.

"I'm afraid, not. I'm fine, but I got a call from Sandra's phone. Some asshole got to her and get this—he wants me to step down. There'll be someone to deliver my phone to you in a few minutes. I trust you to get what you need from there, and trace Sandra's phone."

"Where are you calling me from now?"

I don't even have to say it. Not the time.

"Forget about that. I'll wait for that delivery. I'll get back to you as soon as possible."

"Thank you. And...if you could come over later?"

"I'll see what I can do." Her voice is kind, patient. It occurs to me that it's the voice of someone who will deliver bad news, sooner or later, and that she has done this a few times. I'm not naïve. I know that Sandra's chances aren't good. But if this guy is looking for a fight, I'm going to take it to him.

A bold move. I can put up, especially now that I have friends in high places.

But my old friends will help too, make no mistake.

Claudia is first to arrive. She looks worried, and I almost tell her to cut it out. I'm worried enough for all of us—but this is not her fault.

"How could this happen?"

"I don't know. I imagine he was watching her. Why Sandra? It seems random, but then again, she's the CFO. I guess that's symbolic to someone like him."

"Hm. What are you going to do about it?"

The door opens softly, and Sue lets in Elena and Sofia.

I answer without repeating Claudia's question to the two of them, because the subject of our conversation couldn't be more obvious.

I'm terrified I might have blown it already. I should have asked for a sign of life, then again, no matter what Robyn and her colleagues imagined, this isn't business as usual.

"First of all, I called Robyn and asked her to trace Sandra's phone. I hope that by the time he gets back to me, we have a location."

"And then what?" Sofia asks.

"Then we'll get her out, and...Whatever happens, happens. I'm not going to take any bait. It will be on my terms." I have to save face, in front of him, in front of them. Sofia, of course, sees through me. I wouldn't expect anything else.

"We, what exactly does that mean? We all go to confront him?" Elena asks. "You're sure you don't know who he is?"

"Someone who wants what I have, which could be a lot of people. He asked me to step down, because...A woman in charge of the family obviously offends his petty little self."

"Too bad you can't just send Jimmy like the old days...You know what I mean," Claudia adds quickly. "Not that he was ever trustworthy, but it might be a good idea to replace him."

"I like to believe I already have, with someone far better, and trustworthy."

"Does she know it yet?"

"I think she understood what the introduction to the family meant," Sofia says calmly. "We'll have to wait for the results she brings us and go from there. With a little luck, they'll arrest that man soon."

I'm not sure if that's what I had in mind, but I appreciate her calm focus.

"Sandra is all that matters here. I won't let anyone mess with my employees."

That might not have come out the way I wanted it to. All of them understand what's at stake though. Including Robyn. You can't let these guys walk all over you, or they'll do it again and again.

Capo dei capi doesn't just mean hosting decadent family dinners. It means to take responsibility.

I jump when the phone rings again. It's the entitled asshole kidnapper, ranting on about how I dishonored my family and all families.

"You've had enough time," he says. "What's your answer?"

"It's not that easy. I'm not sure you know, but Sofia is CEO now. Technically I wouldn't step down from anything. I'll have to talk to her."

"Stop bullshitting me. You just paraded your wife in front of your clan. To show everyone who's in charge, huh? Not anymore, Princess."

"It doesn't work that way," I say, aware of the three women watching me. "How do I know you won't kill her anyway?"

"You don't."

"No. I need a sign of life right now, and I need her back unharmed."

I hear a yelp in the background. That, and something else. A train? There aren't any tracks anywhere near the center of the city. Where did he take her?

"There's your sign of life. Listen, Princess, you're in no position to make demands. I, however..."

"Don't listen to him!" Sandra yells on the other end. "He's lying. He—"

The call ends abruptly.

For long, terrifying seconds I don't know what to do. A life depends on me. Many lives depend on me—to do the right things. I have questioned my father's way to make peace, my mother's way to make allies. I feel every bit of the weight they carried on their shoulders, to do right by their loved ones, those who counted on them.

I pick up my phone and call Robyn again.

"Where are we on the trace? He called again."

"I need some more time."

"We don't have that time!" I didn't think I'd raised my voice that much, but the looks on me tell me otherwise.

"I'm sorry, Kendall," Robyn says softly. "I'm going as fast as I can. Do you have any idea?"

"It has to be related to the shooting. Frank, Marla Colvin—I don't know! She can't die. All she ever did was her job!"

"I understand. We are doing the best we can. I promise. I'm sorry, but I have to go back."

"Robyn, please, wait a second." My tone is serious enough to make her reconsider. "Once you have those coordinates, you're going to come to us first." I'm not asking. She hesitates for a few heartbeats.

"Sandra has a wife. Two children. She and her family need to know that I did everything to keep her safe."

"I'll get back to you. Please, trust me," Robyn says before she hangs up.

I only hope I was convincing enough. Meanwhile, I have my own lead to follow.

"Where are train stations around here?" I ask the other women. "Let's get a map."

Chapter Nineteen

Frank Bianco. Marla Colvin. I had done more research on their relationship before Kendall called, hearing Hampton in my mind complaining how it's all a "soap opera."

But Hampton isn't here right now, and neither is SAC Carr.

I heard everything Kendall said between the lines when she asked me to bring the information to her. Truth be told, I knew that day would come after the night of too much champagne and intimacy that was...out of bounds.

I said yes. I said I do.

I have options. One of them means to cross a line from which I can never come back. I think of my parents, my friends, my career—and then Sandra, the CFO, in the hands of a man who threatened to kill her and still might go through with it. A wife and two kids. Family. Kendall's family. My family.

The House of Mancini isn't going to fall, not today.

The head of the tech department calls me to let me know their progress. They don't know exactly yet where the call to Kendall's cell phone came from but could narrow it down to a triangle that covers the hub where cargo arrives from various states. I ask her to get back to me when she has more specifics, then pick up my car keys and leave the building. I drive straight to the Mancini Group's headquarters.

My days of being a kept woman might come sooner than I expected.

I meet several employees on my way from the lobby to the elevators, and up to the top floor, and I can't help but notice the change. At some point, I was the agent overseeing the company's transition to full transparency and legality. They were polite, but cautious. Every big change could mean their job was in danger. But I am Kendall's wife now, initiated into the highest echelon without showing a warrant first.

They're still polite, but there's something else—almost reverence. Like Kendall's family, they have accepted her in her position, and by proxy, they're doing the same for me.

People love a love story. Alphonso and Angela's. Kendall and Robyn's. But before we can think of grandchildren playing at *Catania*, we need to avert a catastrophe.

"The data isn't one hundred percent conclusive yet," I say. "But we're fairly sure Sandra is somewhere in this area. I'm sorry, it's the best we can do for now. I can have a team over there within fifteen minutes."

"Hold that thought." Kendall who has been staring at the map with a frown, straightens. "I thought I heard a train when he called. But with all those cargo trains coming in, it will be hard to identify the exact location."

"What is the plan?" I ask. "I need to know. It would be better if you don't interfere with our operation. We'll have a better chance of finding her."

"You haven't been able to narrow it down, have you? I'm sorry," she apologizes right away.

"Earlier you said taking Sandra specifically might be a metaphor. The location where they are holding her, you think it's related to the company, something your parents might have mentioned at some point?"

She shakes her head. "I can't think of anything. It's driving me crazy that I couldn't identify him. If he thinks he has the sliver of a chance to take over, I *should* know who he is."

I'm tempted to agree with her. Organized crime is a small incestuous world. Not that she's part of that anymore. She would be if there was another revenge execution, but I'm here to help avoid that, aren't I?

"The tech department is going to get back to me when they know more. Meanwhile...cargo trains. It must be more than just a convenient hideout. Let's look at the businesses. Who has the most traffic over there?"

"Some of our supplies come through this place. I know it's a big quantity. I'm not sure how much compared to other companies."

A quick Internet search turns up a virtual map, and businesses close to the hub. It's a reach...It could be anyone hiding behind that phone, though not everyone had access to Sandra or her schedules.

"Who would know her routines, besides you, her family, and the people working under her?"

That earns me a frown. "You think I have a mole in my company?"

"I remember this one driver."

I don't have to go into details in front of the other women. Kendall's expression tells me she knows what I'm referring to, the night a sexy getaway turned into a nightmare, and the end of Jimmy's career with the Mancinis.

"It's impossible. I cleaned up after that."

"Money's an incentive for many. Is there anyone who could even dream about challenging you on that scale? Someone local who isn't in prison or awaiting trial?"

My question hangs in the air as we once again study the map.

"Marrick Enterprises," Elena says out loud. "I heard that name before. Luca mentioned it a few times...Something concerning the Adria restaurants."

And here we have the connection to Adria, perhaps Steve Peck, and that other lead.

"It belongs to *Marla Colvin*," Claudia and I say at the same time.

"Marla and Rick, Marrick." Claudia shakes her head while Kendall looks on, impatient.

"That's him, the fucker who took Sandra? What could he even hope to achieve?"

"Marla was feeding us leads. She had no intention of teaming up with Frank Bianco for anything. It's her husband, Rick Tanner. If we dig deeper, I'm sure we can come up with a connection to Peck."

Claudia shakes her head as realization dawns. "Makes me wonder what the motivation for her relationship with Frank really was. It must have pissed her off that Kendall got ahead of her, delivering Frank to the FBI before they could make a move."

The pieces are coming together. From the beginning, the two of them have been vying for power, trying to set up Frank Bianco along the way. He would have been a convenient scapegoat, but Kendall and I got to him first.

"I have to contact the office," I say. "Get a warrant for Marrick Enterprises."

"No," Kendall says.

"No? Wait a second."

"Try to lean on Marla, have her give up the location. I can't do that because I might cross a line. Meanwhile, I'll deal with Tanner."

"Kendall, no, I can't let you do that. It's too dangerous—for you, and for Sandra."

None of this is at all surprising.

"Send someone else to interrogate Marla, then, and come with me. Please. It's important that I do this."

I could be mad at her, for some good reasons, but the truth is, I already set myself up for this. Not just when I left the office earlier to bring sensitive information to this group—or when I married her. I know that I won't be able to do this balancing act forever, and at the moment, I don't care. If we can save Sandra's life, nothing else matters.

"I'll send someone over to Marla's," I say. "And I'll ask for a team. Then we go."

To my relief, Kendall doesn't protest. The reason I would like her to stay far away from all of this is not just about establishing hierarchy, but about my own selfish fear.

She's Kendall Mancini, and she'll do things her way anyway. I'll do everything I can to keep her from getting hurt.

Chapter Twenty

There are times when the tug of war between us is sensual, and teasing. This is not one of those moments. I have to do what I can, to save Sandra above all, but also to save my status—because if we get this wrong, every asshole with an agenda will try something. I made it clear to my family, and it needs to be clear to the likes of Rick Tanner as well. We don't tolerate any of this.

Regardless, I need to trust Robyn, trust that she's doing the right thing for a woman in danger, and that she's by my side. On my side.

I'm sitting in the car next to her, on our way to Marrick Enterprises. So far, so good.

"Thank you," I say.

"Don't thank me yet." She's not kidding, and I understand why. This is a precarious situation—for Sandra, for us. For Rick Tanner, because he'll understand, too, without a doubt, where he went wrong.

"I mean it. For being here with me." Technically she's the onc driving, but we don't have time for semantics.

"For better or worse. Kendall..." She hesitates.

"I'm listening."

"I hope you are. There will likely be a moment where we have to act, and fast. I know you have a vision of how this will go down, but we can't put the team, or Sandra, in more danger than necessary. You'll do as I say. I'll probably get some flack for bringing you anyway—this is not a regular consultant's assignment."

"I figured. Don't worry. You know what you're doing, I'm aware. You trust me to do the same?"

Conveniently, she has to stop at a red light. Robyn holds my gaze for a long moment.

"Let's bring her home," she says.

Before we get out of the car, Robyn checks in with Agent McKay who went to talk to Marla Colvin. As expected, she's cocky and not giving up her husband. I hear him sigh on the other end.

"She still insists that it was all Frank Bianco's plan, from the shooting in the restaurant, to the kidnapping. He never got over Sofia, and what your parents did, yadda yadda."

I snort at that. "Frank never cared about Sofia in the first place, why would he start now?"

"Is that Kendall with you? Robyn, what's going on?"

"We have a team on standby, just waiting for the warrant. I'll call you back," she says, all business, not leaving any room for an argument. Good. I'm not going to justify my presence to him.

"Okay." She turns to me, her gaze serious. "This is the part you won't like, but please, bear with me. We don't want to tip him off. I'll go in, ask a few questions. If there's any reason to do so, I'll alert the team. Best case scenario, we get the warrant soon and we'll turn this place upside down."

"The 'we' being metaphorical, because the warrant doesn't apply to consultants."

"Kendall, please. I'll come back to you as soon as I can. Anything weird happens, you call me."

Before I can argue, she's out of the car and walking towards the front door of Marrick Enterprises in determined strides. She's right, I don't like it—it might not be the worst idea.

It leaves me with some time to spare, the element of surprise.

Robyn didn't want me to go confront Tanner with her. It's perhaps better that way. She didn't say I had to wait in the car either.

It could take a while longer to get that warrant, but meanwhile, Tanner and Colvin will be rattled. They'll know the FBI is watching them.

I get out and walk a few steps in the parking lot behind the buildings. There's a fence, with tracks on the other side of it. The train I heard runs past here.

I take out my phone and call Sandra's. It's ringing for a long time. Perhaps Tanner has turned it off. He's busy with the agent on his doorstep. I'm about to abandon the call when it's answered. For a few seconds, I hear nothing but heavy breathing.

Could it be...?

"Sandra!"

"Kendall, oh my God, it's you. Please hurry. He's going to kill all of us."

All of us? Is she delirious with pain, drugs?

"Where are you?"

"You have to call Robyn. He placed a bomb at the Mancini Group's headquarters. Tanner killed Tom Foster and tried to blame it on the Biancos. That's why your father met with Frank, hurry, Kendall!"

I can't let her go. I can't.

Meanwhile, Robyn is seeing Tanner on her own.

"It's set to go off in less than thirty minutes. Somewhere in the basement." She is crying. "Do something!"

"I'll call you back," I promise. "I'm coming for you."

"You need to save them."

With a heavy heart, I click on the red button and call SAC Rachel Carr.

"Kendall here. Please, don't ask. Robyn needs back-up at Marrick Enterprises. She already asked for a search warrant. And you need to evacuate the head-quarters of the Mancini Group. Rick Tanner has placed a bomb that's set to go off in about twenty minutes."

"On it," she says curtly. "Don't hang up. Where are you?"

I give her the address. "McKay is still with Marla Colvin. She's in on it. You have to let him know too."

"We'll take care of it. Stay where you are, you hear me?"

"Sure. He kidnapped my CFO. I need to call her back. My phone is still with you—her number is in there."

"Then how are you...never mind. Wait for us."

I'm not promising anything but call Sandra back first.

"He left the phone, but he didn't think I'd get free," she says grimly. "I can't get out though. It's a fire safety door, and it's locked."

"Do you know where it is?"

"It was still dark this morning, but it's close to the Marrick building. Some sort of storage facility at the cargo station." The signal is getting weaker. Damn it. I turn around, trying to find which location would make the most sense. Tanner probably doesn't just have cargo come in—he owns some of those storage facilities.

"Can you think of anything that you saw? They've been tracing your phone, but the area is still too large."

"A door...dark blue or black."

I sigh in relief. The pause was long enough for me to fear I'd lost her.

"Okay, that gives me something to work with. Any-thing else?" In fact, it's still too big an area. But Tanner wouldn't take her far, would he? And he'd have to make sure that not too many people would access the place. I walk away from the Marrick building and towards the cargo station, running past buildings. No blue or black door. Could she have been mistaken?

There, I finally see it.

"Sandra? I think I found it. Stay away from the door."

"Done."

I aim at the lock and take one precise shot. The lock falls to the floor, and I open the heavy door and rush in. Sandra who had hidden behind some crates, struggles to her feet.

"Kendall, I'm so glad to see you!" She winces when I pull her into a quick hug, and for a few seconds, I see red.

"Can you walk?"

"I'm okay. What about headquarters?"

"I notified the FBI. They know how to do this."

"Not too bad to have a direct line," she says wryly. "I hope everyone's going to be okay. This guy is nuts. He thinks he has waited all this time, and—"

"And now it's time to take what is mine."

I spin around to face a man that I've seen a couple of times. He came around to talk to Dad about business. I remember him now, and I remember what my parents said about him. An opportunist, not to be taken seriously, not to be trusted.

"Others have tried before, and you know where that got them."

"Others didn't have the guts to do what needed to be done," he says. "Say goodbye, Princess."

"Down!" I yell at Sandra as I pull the trigger. There's another equally deafening sound, not an echo, but another gunshot.

Robyn holsters her gun as she comes inside.

"They found the bomb," she says. "Everyone got out safely."

"Thank you." I reach out a hand to help up Sandra. "She needs an ambulance."

"Outside," Robyn says. She leans down to check on Tanner, then shakes her head. "Come with me."

Meanwhile, her team has arrived, and so have the paramedics who immediately check on Sandra. After making sure that she is taken care of, I follow Robyn out of the building, the warm sun on my face an odd contrast to the chill still gripping me. This could have gone so many ways. Robyn is silent, and I think I know why.

"I know what you're going to say."

"No, you don't. You did the right thing."

I'm speechless for a heartbeat or two. This is not what I expected.

"I know it was an impossible choice," she continues, "but you acted quickly, and we were able to keep everyone safe. Tanner's secretary lied, by the way. She said he wasn't there while he snuck out through some backdoor. He was going to kill Sandra."

"And me, don't forget that." My attempt at humor falls predictably flat.

"Don't worry, I'll never forget that." She looks down at the gun on her hip.

"There's going to be an investigation." I'm taking an educated guess.

"I might turn this in for good."

"What? I mean, you're serious about that? Wait, that didn't come out right. If that's what you want, I'm one hundred percent behind you. I will testify though if you need me. He had his finger on the trigger."

"Yes, I know. But that's not all."

"What is 'all'?" I should have known that this was not the right time and place.

"I have to talk to a few people now. I'll be home late."

I'm not sure I understand.

"I imagine Rachel will want me to come in for a statement?"

"I'll hold her off until tomorrow. Go home. Get some rest. We'll talk later."

"Are you going to be okay?"

She smiles wryly. "I'll be glad to know you're safe at home."

"Okay. I can do that. But I'll need to drop by the office first."

"I guess you have to. How about I'll let you know when I'm on my way and we order in? *Catania*?"

"Sounds great." In fact, it's beyond strange to discuss dinner options at the scene of a kidnapping, and a shooting—however "good" that shoot may have been—but I sense that we'll have some serious subjects to tackle later. "I'll wait for your call," I say and pull her close for a brief moment.

I watch her walk away, thinking that now that the danger is past, I might call the special number again to arrange a getaway for the two of us. Whatever Robyn decides, we won't back down from a challenge. That doesn't mean we can't have a small time-out from it all. I can't wait to be home with her, but I, too, have work to do first.

I take the back entrance to avoid the press swarming the front doors of headquarters. Law enforcement personnel is still on the scene, and an officer asks me for ID.

"It's all right. That's my company the asshole wanted to blow up. Everyone is back inside?"

"Yes, Ma'am."

"Thank you for keeping everyone safe," I say. Minutes later, I'm in the elevator. The short polite exchange seems to have robbed me of my last energy. It worked out. We didn't lose Sandra. We didn't lose dozens of people today just because one small petty man wanted to play God. Reach for the coveted title.

I didn't lose. I won.

I still don't know what Robyn wants to talk about, but should we go back to the subject we approached the other day, her job situation, it won't be fun and teasing. I wasn't kidding when I said I'd be behind her, no matter what the decision is.

I find Sofia in her office and hug her briefly.

"I'm so relieved everyone is okay."

"Me too. My phone isn't staying quiet for a second. Everyone wants to know how you averted a catastrophe."

I shake my head, not ready for that interpretation. "All I did was to pass on some information. I was, we were all lucky the FBI could act on it right away...What?"

"Let's have a coffee," she suggests. "Sit, please. Let me tell you something. This is an important moment. Don't make yourself small."

"Small? I was scared out of my mind."

"Yeah, I know what that's like, but look at us now. I'm going to call the kitchen for some snacks."

"That sounds really good." I'm almost surprised to find my voice this brittle, but given the company, I don't mind.

Chapter Twenty-One

I had a speech prepared when I walked into Rachel Carr's office, but when I sit across from her in the visitor's chair, the words don't come easily. I had many goals and dreams when I first came to work for this office. But dreams change. Priorities change.

"What's this?" she asks, and I put the envelope I brought with me in front of her.

"I have given this a lot of thought, and I've come to realize that there's no other solution. I am resigning."

Rachel doesn't look surprised. I don't know if that's a good or a bad thing. If anything, she had to know that the situation was always beyond complicated for me.

"I'm not a quitter," I continue. "But something needs to change. Today taught me that more than anything."

"I can't say I didn't expect this at all, but I thought we'd talk about Kendall's consultancy first."

"It makes sense to keep her on. She's helpful."

"That she is. So are you. I trusted the decisions you made. For what it's worth, about Rick Tanner...You had no choice. The report will state just that. You could take some time and come back when you're ready."

"Thank you, but no. I'm not going to change my mind."

She looks like she's struggling with that fact, surprise, or no surprise. I'm past struggling. I know who I am. The truth has never been so clear to me.

"Robyn, if you need anything, don't hesitate to call. I mean it. And never forget that this case made a huge difference for many. A lot of people in the city and beyond are breathing easier."

"I'm glad. Thank you for everything."

I thought I'd leave right away, but then I make a beeline for the break room. This building holds many memories for me, good and bad ones. I'll make new memories. A new start.

Hampton sits at a table with a coffee, frowning over something he's reading. Agent Teresa Lowry stands in a corner checking her phone. She too closed a big case recently though it was a lot more under the radar than the much-covered Mancini story.

Kendall's story. Mine.

Both Hampton and Teresa look up when I come in. Teresa gets to her feet.

"Good luck, Robyn," she says, giving me a quick smile and a pat on the shoulder before she leaves the room.

"So, this is it?" he asks.

"I guess so. Don't be a stranger?"

He shakes his head, frustration radiating off of him as he closes the file soundly.

"It didn't have to end this way. She got to you after all. I never thought that would happen."

I didn't expect him to understand all of it. The accusation still stings. Perhaps I should explain. I don't know if I can.

"A lot of people have been arrested in the past few months."

"Right," he says, sounding skeptical. "So many we could almost close down Organized Crime—but Kendall Mancini wasn't one of them."

"Because she helped us make it happen. I'm not sure what you're thinking, but I'm not some sort of sacrifice, but...I sacrificed all right, and I can't ignore the cost of it all any longer. This is my chance. I'm taking it. I'm sorry if that doesn't fit the image you had of me."

Hampton holds my gaze. "Do you trust her? With your life—or anyone else's?"

I think of all the recent information I have received, everything I have learned. Kendall's business is beyond reproach these days. At the same time, she will not hesitate to protect the ones she loves. This is as crystal clear to me as is the necessity for me to take this step.

"Yes," I say without hesitation. "I love her. I know she hasn't always played by the rules, but that's over. Some might think she doesn't deserve that wealth, or even her freedom, but she's doing a lot of good with it. I don't want to miss another moment."

My words hang in the air for long, uncertain moments, before he gets up and moves to embrace me. "Good luck. I'm sorry about what you went through with Dolan."

"Thanks."

I disengage myself and leave the room before the moment gets too emotional. I might have a few of them ahead of me.

—ele—

I arrive at the condo later that afternoon, finding the dining room table set for two. Kendall greets me with an embrace, holding on tightly, which is good because I'm nervous. I shouldn't be. Earlier with Hampton, and Rachel Carr, I sounded convinced—and convincing. With Kendall, I've only talked about this as an unrealistic, last resort. We both followed in our family's footsteps, we do what we love, and there's no straying from the plan—or is there?

Is there ever a way out when the price becomes too high? There has to be. Everyone deserves to be happy.

"I resigned," I say. "Please, don't say you're going to divorce me. I'll continue to work, in the company or somewhere else if you prefer that, but I thought you should know—"

"Please, sit." Her tone is as soft as her touch when she takes my hand and leads me over the couch by the floor to ceiling windows. "You know you have a job in the company if you want it. You can start tomorrow, or whenever you're ready."

"Just like that? Without an explanation?"

"I didn't say that," she says, making me laugh. "You'll tell me when you feel like it, though I could take a few educated guesses."

"Maybe we don't always need to know everything."

"Maybe there's a perfect time for revelations."

The tears feel hot on my face. So many regrets. I don't want to live like that anymore. I don't want to miss any more chances.

"I'm proud of what we achieved together. I'm sorry I had to lie to you to make it happen."

"Yet I asked you to move in with me and marry me. I think I got over it." When this doesn't get the intended reaction, she continues, more serious, "I was consumed. By the need to avenge my parents, to hold up a façade, by the responsibility to make sure everyone had what they needed. You helped me channel all that rage in a different way—I'm not sure you'll ever know how much that means to me. It may sound trite, but who cares. You made me a better person. You also made me smarter—because obviously most of my family knew how to take care of themselves."

When I came home earlier, I didn't expect a passionate speech like that. It makes me think of the first time I saw her. We will never be able to ignore certain realities, the way we started out, the lines we crossed.

We found something that's stronger, something that will help us both through the recent challenges and trauma.

"I love you," I say, and this time it's without reservation or double meaning.

"I love you too." She barely has time to finish the sentence before my lips find hers in a passionate, take no prisoners kiss. I know I did the right thing. I won't be a kept woman either, but we'll guard each other's secrets—and we won't take those second chances for granted.

We're halfway out of our clothes when the doorbell rings. With a frustrated sound, Kendall straightens her dress and gets up.

"That's our dinner."

She walks to the door barefoot, as I, too, make myself presentable.

I'm not done crying. We're not done talking or using intimacy to postpone those conversations for a bit longer, but this is a start.

It's the start of the new life.

Chapter Twenty-Two

I know that Robyn has wrestled with this decision, and that she didn't take it lightly. In an ironic twist of fate, I will still be connected to the FBI, but that doesn't matter now.

I vowed to give her everything she needed. In the short term. In the forever after.

The delivery person interrupted my first attempt. We'll put that on hold for a while in favor of food.

Not just any food.

Food from *Catania* that always comes with a bit of magic, to heal the soul. Turns out we both need a lot of healing. It's a start.

Halfway through the meal, I can see her eyes are still bright with unshed tears. The end of this case, the end of her employment with the FBI, it has got to bring up a lot of memories. For sure, she hadn't planned any of this when she walked into that bar to make first contact. And maybe she's thinking of Elaine Driver who left after an incident that was traumatic for both of them.

"I'm sorry."

"No need to be. It's been tough for a long time. I can relate."

"I'm sorry about all the detours, and every time I needed to keep things from you."

"Again, I've done the same..."

She pauses, takes a sip of her wine. "I know, and there were times we couldn't avoid it, but we made choices. We chose us."

"We did," I agree.

"Tanner and Colvin were out of their minds. They thought they could take over, from you, from the Biancos...I don't understand women like Colvin," she confesses. "She was one of the masterminds behind the plan, but she would never get any credit had it worked out."

"Except for a luxury life from blood money. Some women don't mind that," I remind her and cringe, hard.

"Don't worry. I know you're not talking about me."

"I'm not. Don't get me wrong. If someone hurts those close to me, they're always going to pay."

Robyn holds her breath for a heartbeat, perhaps wondering if I'm going to make revelations of my own. I might. Someday. She knows the lengths I'm willing to go to keep her safe. Without a doubt, that played into her decision.

"But I think I'm going to keep my consultant job," I continue. "Keep in touch with my new friends." In reality, they're neither friends nor enemies, but it might be beneficial to keep them close for a little while longer. "I won't lie—I enjoyed seeing Frank and his clan going to jail. Luca, not so much, but I certainly learned who in my family wants to keep things clean. I'll make sure he's okay. Whether he likes it or not."

"Are we going to be okay?" she asks.

"You want the short answer or the long one? The short answer is yes."

"Then we can stop here."

"Let me just tell you something. We will be okay. You're right, we've achieved a lot. Right now, we're perhaps seeing the most stability we've ever had in the city. It's good for business, it's good for everyone else. There might be someone reaching for that power again, and they will fail."

"Because you managed to do what your father wanted to do before they got to him," she concludes. "You're *Capo dei capi* now. What does that make me?"

"My partner in everything." Her expression is calm, interested. It's not news to her, whether we use certain labels or not. Peck was wrong about her—Robyn has and will have a lot more power than he could ever imagine, no matter what career she chooses.

"Is that true?"

"It's been true for some time now. We might have been a bit more creative than previous generations...but it's what it's always been. My mother didn't always work in the company. Even though I was born into the family, I had to find my place. You have yours."

"It sounds so easy when you say it."

"It will be as easy as we make it." I take her hand in mine. "I promise you."

—ele—

I'm aware that a luxury retreat might not solve the grief and loss Robyn still needs to process or make the challenges that lie ahead any less difficult. No, I'm taking her because we both earned it, and the last time, we were rudely interrupted.

Sofia will take good care of things meanwhile.

I sat down with Claudia and Marc, warning them that there could be no more deviations. We are in this together now, and for the future. I left them to work out whatever it is they need to work out.

Luca is working hard to get back in my good graces. I visit him regularly, and the conversations we've been having are encouraging. It will take some time before he can hope to perhaps get out on good behavior, but when he does, there will be a place for him at the family table. He has apologized to Robyn too. Elena divorced him and decided to move back to her hometown. Luca's boyfriend is waiting for him.

I still work with Carr on an occasional basis, and we agree that maintaining a certain equilibrium is good for everyone.

Finally, Robyn and I will go on that retreat, but before that, we'll have dinner with her parents. The past few months have flown by, and so we couldn't always make the time.

But this is important too. The equilibrium.

"Your parents believed in tradition," Blake says when the two of us somehow end up alone in the den. Coincidence, not because I always demanded to sit with the "men of the house." It's not a coincidence that he mentions my parents in this context. I listen.

"At first, they really thought that Jimmy was a good match. He was a pretty good actor, fooled everyone."

Where is he going with this?

"I hate to say it, but for some time, he fooled me too. I'm glad that it's over, and I'm sure my parents would be too."

"Yes. Above all, they wanted you to be happy. It's what we want for Robyn, too."

"I can imagine." I look him straight in the eye. "I have the same aspirations for the family we're going to have."

He acknowledges everything I said with a wry smile.

"I should have told you that when you got married, and I'm sorry I didn't. I'm glad Robyn found you."

"Thank you. That means a lot."

It seems like everyone has come around. From here, we're nearly invincible, aren't we?

Robyn and her mom walk into the room, each of them carrying their drinks. I can tell from the excited spark in her mother's eyes that Robyn told her about the plans we've made.

Tradition, family, love, we have all of it, no matter who tried to take it from us.

You don't mess with a Mancini, ever.

Epilogue

"Can we have ice cream? Please?" Blake pleads.

I feign hurt. "What, you don't want to try grandma's cannoli?" He looks uncertain for a moment, and Angela laughs.

"Come on, Mom, don't do that. You know that these two are your best customers in the ice cream shop."

"I guess that's true. All right, let's get you some. What's the flavor of today?"

"Chocolate," he says with all due reverence. For the ice cream, not his elders, but that's all right. Our grandson has his priorities and heart in the right place, just like his twin sister.

"How about ice cream *and* cannoli?"

"You are tough negotiators," I ascertain. "Let's see what we can do."

On our anniversary, *Catania* is bursting at the seams with family and friends who came to honor Robyn and me, and the consistently out-of-this-world food. Across the room I see retired SAC Carr. We are maintaining that equilibrium.

Robyn and I are still involved in the Mancini Group, still calling the shots though our daughter Angela will be ready to take over whenever it's necessary. Her wife, Naomi, is running *Catania* and the new ice cream parlor.

Business is good.

After everyone is satisfied with their dessert options, I pick up a bottle of champagne and find Robyn to refill her glass.

She surveys the room full of people, adults talking and laughing, children calming down for a brief moment as they're enjoying their sweet treat.

"Is this what you always dreamed of?"

I don't have to think about it for a moment. We have faced many challenges. We never backed down, never ran—and we don't intend to, no matter how well Dad meant with that "college fund."

"You know it is. What about you?"

She leans in until her lips meet mine.

"I was obsessed with you from the moment I met you. That has never changed—and it never will. Happy anniversary."

Not so bad for someone who started out with no friends—I'm surrounded by friends and family now, and I found the best thing: The happily ever after.

About the Author

Barbara Winkes writes suspense and romance with lesbian characters at the center. She has always loved stories in which women persevere and lift each other up. Expect high drama and happy endings. Women loving women always take the lead.

www.barbarawinkes.wordpress.com

Acknowledgments

This trilogy would not exist without Dominique who helps me shape my stories so they make sense, May Dawney's extraordinary cover art, and readers who were intrigued by a sapphic mafia romance and took the journey with Kendall and Robyn.

Thank you so much!

www.ingramcontent.com/pod-product-compliance
Lightning Source LLC
Chambersburg PA
CBHW022024170626
46808CB00003B/1049